PROFESSIONAL DEVELOPMENT

THE BENCHMARKS SERIES

KATE CANTERBARY

VESPER PRESS

 Created with Vellum

ABOUT PROFESSIONAL
DEVELOPMENT

Tara Treloff and Drew Larsen hate each other.

They *really* hate each other.

This would be fine except for the issue of them sharing
a job title
…and an office
…and now a five-hour-long drive to a conference their
boss has made mandatory to resolve their issues a few
days before Christmas.

And they would've been able to muddle through all of
those matters but a major snowstorm is heading
their way
…and there's only one bed.

CHAPTER ONE

TARA

"BANANAS," Drew snapped, glaring across the conference table at me while he did it.

Of course he'd safe-word out of this conversation.

"Give me three minutes." I matched his glare. "You won't be begging "bananas" when I'm done."

And of course I thought of our back-on-track trigger as a safe word. That was how it worked. Someone said "bananas" during a meeting only when the conversation had strayed out of bounds and into off-topic territory. "Bananas" kept our school leadership team meetings structured, specific, and constructive.

Not so different from safe, sane, and consensual.

Yep, that was my train of thought. There was no shutting down my dirty mind and I couldn't see a reason why shutting it down was necessary. This wasn't the olden days when teachers were fired for getting married and—gasp!—*having* sex. Headmasters didn't take bullshit vows of celibacy and the good ones didn't hang with that icky, antiquated title either.

I was allowed my dirty mind as long as I didn't cross the line from professional into pervy by actually calling it a safe word during a school day.

"I'm not giving you three minutes," Drew gritted out. "I said bananas. This is over. Your calibration of oral reading fluency probes is irrelevant to our agenda and I'm not wasting three minutes on that when we have campus-wide priorities to address." With a dismissive flick of his wrist, he brushed me and my argument aside. "Keep your early elementary issues where they belong, Miss Treloff."

That obnoxious fucker. As if he got a pass on his obnoxious fuckery because he capped it off with *Miss Treloff.*

"As I'm sure you're well aware, *Mr. Larsen*," I said, my words sharpened to a point, "plenty of *your* upper elementary students struggle with oral reading fluency."

"They wouldn't if you'd done your job effectively," he said, as matter-of-fact as today's fucking weather.

Yeah, I had a dirty mind and I used *fuck* like it was a comma. It was a damn good thing I knew how to keep that shit in my head rather than blasting it at the obnoxious fucker sitting across from me. I'd wanted to unload the fires of hell upon this douche canoe every day for the past two years.

That I could sit here and take his shit was all the proof I needed to know I was better than his Ivy League, bearded-up, buttoned-down, condescending bullshit.

And I *had* to be better. I poured actual sweat and tears into my work as co-dean of Bayside School. I did that because I loved my job and I believed in this work, but there was no way in hell I'd let my counterpart Drew Larsen win.

"Unnecessary, Drew." Lauren Halsted-Walsh, the school's founder and principal, didn't look up from her notebook to shut down my nemesis. "We can probably save the ORF conversation for our literacy data meeting tomorrow, Tara."

Drew gave me his favorite *I was right and you were wrong* face, a smarmy smirk that made him look more like a rotting jack-o'-lantern than a thirty-four-year-old man.

I preferred the rotting jack-o'-lantern. It suited my co-dean far more than the unfortunately beautiful package in which he existed. Honestly, he was undeserving of the entire high cheeked, chiseled jaw, broad shouldered, pouty lipped situation—not to mention the very tall, very dark, very handsome side of the equation.

More importantly, it was unfair to the human population which was often drawn to his arrestingly hot appearance and led to believe he was someone worth knowing.

He was not. He was a pompous dickhead who happened to be good enough at his job to make up for his burnt toast personality.

"That works," I said to her, smiling. "I'm sure Drew won't mind us making decisions about the assessment methods that impact all students receiving literacy intervention next quarter."

I crossed my arms, shot him a smug smile. Another battle in my win column.

He muttered under his breath as he glanced away and tossed an irritated glare toward the window. "If that's the case," he started, slowly shifting his attention back toward me, "you should've included it in the agenda beforehand. Ad hoc additions violate the norms of our meeting protocol and as I stated earlier"—he leaned forward, sneering at the sunflower doodles on my copy of the meeting's agenda—"are bananas."

That fucker and his safe word. That *fucking fucker*.

"As I'm sure you're capable of noticing, the agenda has—"

Lauren shook her head, stopping my argument, and jumped in with, "We've now dedicated more time to procedural discussion than actual content and we cannot extend our time this morning. I have a hard stop at ten thirty." She closed her notebook, laced her fingers together on top of it. "I couldn't help but notice you two are still struggling to establish a working relationship that isn't smothered by your shared resentment of each other."

"Our working relationship is fine when we don't have to interact," I said. "Drew keeps to his half of the building, I keep to mine, and everything is great."

"Except my half of the building inherits the students from your half of the building," Drew argued. "It would help if they rolled into fourth grade having mastered third grade standards."

"You know damn well the vast majority of last year's third graders were at or above grade level at the end of the year," I said.

He shrugged. "But not all, Tara."

"No, not *all*, Drew," I replied. Was this how it felt for blood to boil? Was this it, the overwhelming sense I was going to turn cherry red and blast out of my seat in rage? "It will never be one hundred percent and the fact you believe it's attainable is the root of our problem."

Nodding, he said, "Allow me to acknowledge that, for once, you're right. It is the root of our problem. I expect more and so should you."

"Porcupines," Lauren said, using the one trigger more powerful than bananas. It was a time-out, red card, and veto all in one, and she'd only used it once before. She held up her hands, breaking apart this argument. "It's clear you both have strong opinions about effective school leadership and it's one of the things I admire about each of you. That these opinions differ only makes them more meaningful. The challenge I've wanted you to tackle since it became clear we needed to cleave the dean role into two—"

"I still disagree with that," Drew muttered.

She leveled him with a glare and I took immense joy in watching the arrogant glint in his eyes cool. "*Porcupines*," she repeated.

"Excuse me," he replied, staring at the table. "My bad."

It was absurdly unfair how good he looked while brooding over that verbal smackdown. Like a modern-day Dracula, turning up his coat collar to protect himself from the discomforts of this world.

Not unlike Dracula, Drew sucked the life out of everything around him.

"Since this role was split and Tara was selected to lead the early elementary side, I've hoped you two would shift on those differences," Lauren continued. "Not abandoning them but coming together in service to those differences."

"That was my hope for this work too," I said, not at all above sucking up to my boss. Dirty mind aside, I was nothing if not a teacher's pet. "Though I'm not sure we're able to do that"—I spared a glance at my moody, chastened nemesis—"when these differences are fundamental."

They were also elitist horseshit. My counterpart seemed to think his Ivy League education—Dartmouth, and he wouldn't let you forget it—meant he was the most intelligent person in any room.

But Drew's degree wasn't in education or child development. Not even math, the subject he'd taught for five years before helping Lauren open this school. Nope, Drew had studied philosophy and—*allegedly*—stumbled into the classroom.

Because that made any sense at all.

I, on the other hand, had degrees in both child development *and* early childhood education. I was fully qualified for my work, even if I'd studied at low-ranking state schools.

"I hear what you're saying and I know you believe it and feel it," Lauren replied. "But I know you two. I *chose* you two. And I know you're more aligned than you think." She pulled a file folder out from under her laptop, handed papers from it to us. "That's why I want you to attend this training session. Registration closed six months ago and the wait list was a nightmare, but I made some calls and swapped with a few other school leaders to secure seats for you."

"This...this is in upstate New York," Drew murmured, frowning at the paper.

"And it's next week. It's right before holiday break," I added.

"We'll be off campus the last two days of the term," Drew said.

"Correct," Lauren replied. "You'll have plenty of time on the drive to and from Albany to make sense of those differences."

Drew dropped the paper as if it was poison. "You want us to—*what?*"

"There's no reason for you to drive separately," she said, her words slapping in their finality. "Look, I know it's short notice but it's not as though we had anything critical taking place those days. You know, I am capable of keeping things under control by myself for a bit. The last two days before winter holiday break are a fine time to step away and then come back strong in the new year. Strong *together*."

I put the paper down, flattened my palms over it. "I am looking forward to this," I managed. "I'm excited—I am—but I'm also concerned that we won't be able to accomplish all this in two days, Lauren." I met Drew's gaze, silently willing him to agree with me. Instead, he arched an eyebrow and left me to hoe this row alone.

Dammit, I was always hoeing alone. "These goals seem ambitious for the timeline."

"You should give it a try," Drew quipped. "See what you're made of."

That fucker.

With an impatient sigh, Lauren glanced at the clock above her door and then back at us. "It is ambitious and I expect you'll make a concerted effort," she said. "If you're not able to make meaningful progress, I'll have no choice but to reevaluate this staffing model. I believe in you both but this holy war has to end. It's not productive and it's not the best use of your skills and talents. And honestly, mediating isn't the best use of *my* skills and talents. We have better things to do and it's time we do them."

My stomach sank to my toes. Drew wasn't going anywhere. He wasn't going to be reevaluated out of a job. Despite the obvious fact he was an egotistical jerk with unforgiving standards and a burgeoning god complex, the teaching staff *adored* him. His tentacles were wrapped around this school and they had been since the very first day. If anyone was leaving, it was me.

The smirk he shot me confirmed it. He'd wanted me gone and now it seemed his wish was coming true. He'd never see my perspective and there was no way in hell I was bending to his.

"Ten thirty." Lauren pointed at the clock. "Unless you want to talk while I pump, this is where we adjourn." She stood, fetched her breast milk pumping kit from under her desk. Her baby daughter was about six months old and an adorable little meatball. "Tell your teams you'll be unavailable those days. I'll forward digital copies of the training and hotel information to you. I'll leave it up to you to figure out your travel plans." She unzipped the bag and set an empty bottle on the table. *"Together."*

Drew pushed to his feet, his gaze cast toward the ceiling, as if scandalized by the sight of the bottle. "Understood," he said, heading toward the door without a backward glance.

"Yeah," I murmured, still reeling from Lauren's gently issued ultimatum.

This was an independent lab school, an incubator for new educational innovation. We got to test out history textbooks that didn't limit the world to western Europe, and new apps for learning foreign languages, and we welcomed researchers into our classrooms every day. But my contract provided no layers of bureaucracy between me and unemployment.

"We'll, uh, we'll get it together," I added.

She gave me a crisp grin. "Yes. You will."

"Thank you for making this happen. Getting us into the training," I added.

"You can thank me when you get back." There was warmth in her words, but it was severe.

I gathered my things and shuffled out, Lauren hot on my heels as she locked the door and pulled the blinds behind me. My laptop clutched to my chest, I wandered into the teachers' workroom, knowing I'd find Drew there.

There was no reason to seek him out. In fact, this was a waste of my time. I had classrooms to visit and coaching meetings to prepare for, and probably a new job to find. Leaning against the communal lunch table while he slid papers into mailboxes and ignored me completely was not a smart choice.

But I stayed and said, "About this training thing—"

"I'll drive," he interrupted, still busy delivering mail.

"Oh, so, you've just decided that?" I asked.

Goddammit, I should not have picked another fight with him. I should've agreed and skipped this argument altogether. I didn't even like driving but I did enjoy being included in the decision-making when those decisions involved me.

"I have evaluated the facts and reached a conclusion." He was slotting papers into mailboxes like they were darts. "You travel by public transit wherever possible. When you do drive, it's with that charming little girlmobile."

Even if I wanted to, I couldn't fight him on this point. I drove the same poppy red Volkswagen Beetle I'd had for almost thirteen years, all the way back to high school. Red duct tape held the passenger side mirror in place and I had to work my ass off to avoid potholes unless I wanted to crack another rim.

Drew drove a black SUV with tinted windows and all manner of grills and guards and extraneous metal. It screamed, "I'm compensating for something in a *big* way!"

I pursed my lips in disapproval. I didn't care that his back was to me. "And your souped-up manmobile is the answer?"

"In case you're not familiar with the route from Boston to Albany, it's through the Berkshire Mountains. And in case you've forgotten, it's December in the Northeast." He lifted his shoulders, which had the impolite effect of tightening his blue checkered dress shirt across the lean muscles of his back. I glared at those muscles. Did all his clothes have to fit him like...*that?* And his hair, did it have to be dark and wavy? Really? Didn't he have enough? "Higher elevation, winding roads, frequent fog and inclement weather. In this instance, yes, my souped-up manmobile with four-wheel drive and snow tires is the answer."

He finished distributing his papers but didn't turn

around. Instead, he tapped his finger against one of the slots and turned his head to the side, just enough to catch sight of me over his shoulder.

After a moment of silence settled between us, he asked, "Anything else on your mind?"

"I know what you're doing," I snapped, the words sputtering out of me.

He glanced down at the mailboxes. "Please, Tara. Tell me what I'm doing."

The trouble with Drew was that he constantly made his obnoxious fuckery look innocent.

He knew I wasn't comfortable with a long drive on mountain roads so he stepped up to the plate.

He knew logistics wasn't my strength so he took the liberty of scheduling parent-teacher conferences for all grade levels without mentioning it to me until after it was done.

He developed a process for writing and reviewing lesson plans, and shot it off to my team as if I was on board with his plan.

He took it one step too far and he made sure he was the hero every time.

So damn helpful, that Drew Larsen.

"You're making it impossible for me to succeed."

He shook his head once. "It's not my responsibility to level the playing field for you."

A startled laugh shot out of me. "There's something I don't understand about you, Drew."

"Just the one thing? I would've thought you'd have a longer list," he murmured.

Ignoring that quip, I continued, "I don't understand why you think it helps anyone to get rid of me. You're already indispensable. No one will ever dispute that. You're the only person who can fix the basement copier and you know every single student's history offhand and your voice is heard in every big decision around here. As much as you complain about knowing my work better than I do, you don't actually want to dedicate your days to coaching the early elementary teachers on teaching print awareness or base-ten strategies. I'm sorry, but I don't buy that. It would seriously cut into your running-around-and-knowing-every-thing-about-everything time, and where would you be if you didn't take it upon yourself to reinstall a whiteboard because it's hanging slightly askew? Listen, we don't have to love each other but we do need to play for the same team. I'm willing to make the effort if you are."

Drew's lips curled up in a grin that wasn't warm, wasn't kind. He regarded me over his shoulder for a long moment before saying, "Have you been rehearsing that long? The delivery seemed a bit uneven."

I huffed out a breath and pushed away from the table. I hated this guy. "Know this: I'm not letting you win without one hell of a fight."

As I marched toward the door, he called, "You don't have to let me win. I can do it all by myself."

That *fucker*.

CHAPTER TWO

DREW

I COULDN'T RETURN to our office. There was no way I could share that space with Tara right now. Not when I'd have to share an entire road trip with her next week.

Everything about our metro Boston campus was perfect with the crucial exception of not having enough offices to accommodate two deans. The space existed—assuming we relocated one of our speech-language pathologists to a walk-in closet and claimed his small room in the name of our power struggle.

Since neither Tara nor I were willing to compromise the needs of our student services staff in the name of our blood-thick yet petty rivalry, we made do with an office that seemed to shrink by the minute.

It was a decently sized space but with two desks, a tall bookshelf, and a small, round meeting table that we had to push into a corner and only allowed for two chairs, there was no breathing room left. Writing on the whiteboard required leaning across the meeting table and if I didn't push my chair in all the way, we couldn't close the door.

I spent a lot of time away from that space. I observed in classrooms every day, tucked myself away in the art or music rooms when they weren't in use, found reasons to hang out in the main office near Lauren and the nurse. None of those people hated me.

Today, I headed straight for the middle school wing, housing our sixth, seventh, and eighth graders. Most people scrunched up their noses at the notion of working with tweens and preteens but I loved those kids something fierce. It was my favorite age group. I treasured everything about that weird, wonky phase of development.

In that regard, Tara had one truth down cold: I wasn't cut out for early elementary. I'd managed well enough in the years before Lauren decided this job was too big for one person—even though I'd abhorred her noticing I couldn't handle it all—but my strengths lived in upper elementary and middle school.

I slipped into Clark Kerrin's social studies and history class and tucked myself into the kidney-shaped table in the back of the room while he talked through key elements of ancient Olmec society. Because Clark was a pro, he didn't even blink in my direction, instead continuing on with this portion of his lesson.

My laptop open, I created a new document and hammered out a list of things I'd need to do in advance of this Albany trip. My schedule for next Thursday and Friday needed to be shuffled, I'd have to collect my dry cleaning a day earlier than usual, and my car was going to need servicing—just to be on the safe side. And I'd need to figure out how I was going to survive all that time with Tara.

I glanced up when I noticed Clark's voice getting closer.

"I want you to flip back to your notes from last week and draft a list of ways in which the Olmecs and the Greeks were similar in the development of their civilizations," he said to the students when he reached the back table. "Don't forget to check in on architecture and art while you're doing that, please."

I stood, glancing at the sixth graders as they started paging through their notebooks. "They're really into the comparative civilization stuff, aren't they?"

He frowned at the page of notes on my laptop and asked in a low voice, "Am I being formally observed right now?"

"Oh, no, sorry," I said quietly, waving at the screen. While I visited classrooms all the time, I didn't usually sit down and take verbatim notes more than once a quarter. "This is totally unrelated. I just wanted to pop in for a few minutes."

"And flash murderous glares at me while you did it?" he asked, laughing. "You know that's always a fun experience for me."

"My apologies. No murderous vibes intended," I said. "I just needed to avoid…" I shrugged, shoved my hands in my pockets. "You know."

With a knowing nod, he glanced out the door to the classroom directly across the hall where Noa Elbaz was breaking down the ancient Greek myth of Narcissus. She had a roll of blue masking tape dangling from her wrist, three dry erase markers in hand, and two Sharpies clipped to her lanyard.

"Yep," he replied, still watching her. "I know all about it." The moment broke when he clapped me on the back. "If you're staying a bit, would you make yourself useful and go sit by Braxton? He requires some hairy eyeballs to keep him focused on this class rather than his book."

When Clark returned to the front of the room, I pulled a chair up beside Braxton and tapped the mostly empty graphic organizer on his desk. "Get caught up while you can," I said quietly. "You don't want to have to do this at lunch, my friend."

With a stifled groan, he closed the graphic novel

he'd been reading under his desk and set to gathering the information he'd missed. I should've done the same but all I could think about was Tara Treloff.

As if that was anything new.

CHAPTER THREE

DREW

I COULD NEVER DECIDE whether I enjoyed days like these, when the sun was lost behind cold, gray clouds and the air snapped with icy promises of snow. I didn't favor the dismal dreariness but this weather was ripe for getting things done. No one was itching to go outside when it was thirty degrees and windy. There were no autumn leaves, no spring flowers, no summer fun. Days like these were good for focus and quiet.

I preferred the quiet.

As I watched Tara trundling down the school's front steps with her purple roller luggage in tow, I knew I wasn't getting any of it today.

She was going to talk the entire drive. I was sure of it. She'd talk and talk and talk, and I'd rip the steering wheel off or drive into a ditch if a blood vessel in my brain didn't rupture and kill me first. That happened to otherwise healthy thirty-four-year-old men, right?

She was wearing *those* pants too. The ones that drove me mad and had once started me on a campaign to ban all legging-style bottoms in the staff handbook.

I'd lost that campaign and earned myself another "What the hell were you thinking, Drew?" conversation with a side of "And don't you have enough work to do as it is?" with Lauren.

But *those* pants. The slim black ones that made her seem impossibly small, as if she was a doll come to life rather than a woman in her late twenties.

She wore a lot of dresses, the kind that announced her as a former kindergarten teacher in loud shouts. The great blur of color and pattern always made it easier for me to tune out her body like an endlessly pulsing toothache. *Those* pants did not.

No, today she believed it necessary to pair the pants with a petal pink blouse and boots that served only decorative purposes. If she wasn't careful for that slick patch at the end of the sidewalk, she was going to fall on her ass because they looked about as functional as the bright ballet flats she favored.

By my count, she had them in eight different colors. Red, hot pink, orange, yellow, dark green, navy blue, purple, black. The yellow was a recent addition.

In a particularly deranged moment several months

ago, I'd looked up the brand of shoes. It was fully unhinged, not a drop of logic to be found, but I wanted to find out which colors she was missing from her collection.

Now, the internet served me ads for women's shoes more often than anything else. I was on a couple of mailing lists too.

"Have you used the bathroom?" I called from the parking lot. I popped the rear gate on my SUV. "I'm not stopping in an hour because you have the bladder of a kindergartner."

"I'm not answering that," Tara replied, shoving the luggage handle down when she stopped in front of me. "But go right ahead and treat me like I'm five. That will work out well for you."

"I'm not treating you like you're five," I replied because I was physically incapable of letting a single thing go where Tara Treloff was concerned. "I'm treating you like you're a teacher of five-year-olds. We know how teachers mirror their students."

She hefted her luggage and shoved it in the trunk, right beside mine. "By that logic, you're a moody, pubescent tween."

You're not wrong, Miss Treloff. You are not wrong.

I glanced back at the building. Avoidance was essential. It was the only weapon I had left. "Are you sure you don't need to go?"

She huffed out an aggravated sigh as she rounded the SUV and flung open the passenger side door. "Inappropriate, Larsen. Really freakin' inappropriate."

I turned my keys over in my palm, still holding out hope for a last-minute change of plans.

Lauren might decide she needed us here more than she wanted us off site.

The training could be canceled.

Moose could overtake the interstate and grind road travel to a halt.

The eastern seaboard could break off and sink into the Atlantic.

I could stumble into ongoing traffic and lose both legs under the wheels of a tractor trailer.

At this point, welcomed possibilities.

"Are we doing this or what, Larsen?" Tara called from the front seat.

I glanced at her, the rear gate still open. My car was going to smell like her now.

It was bad enough I couldn't walk into our office without getting hit with a wall of vanilla and I couldn't sit through a meeting without drowning in her scent, but now it was in my car.

I couldn't manage that. I'd have to sell the car.

"Drew!" she yelled. "What are you doing? You sent me fifteen reminders about when you wanted to leave and gave me an enormous lecture about timing our departure to avoid rush hour traffic and icy roads. I rearranged my schedule to be here at the exact minute you requested. Stop screwing around back there and let's go."

I didn't respond.

I pressed a button on my key fob and the rear gate closed but I stayed there, rooted on the asphalt while I stared at Tara through the back window as she scraped her long, shiny hair into a bun.

I'd watched her knot her hair around this time every day for the past two years. She always came to school with it loose, the straight espresso strands parted on the left side. She'd arrive with an elastic band on her wrist too. Sometime between lunch and dismissal, the band came off her wrist and she gathered her hair into a tail or twist.

I hated that part of the day. I'd taken to avoiding our office in the afternoon because seeing her fuss with her hair pinched and chafed at me in the worst ways. Why she had to groom herself in our small, shared workspace when we had restrooms was a damn mystery to me.

The hair was one issue but the bottom line was I hated Tara. I hated everything about her. I hated her vanilla scent, her shiny hair, the zany voices she used with kids, the firm, no-bullshit voice she used with adults. I hated how she overflowed with enthusiasm for everything, all the time. I hated that she only used purple or green pens and I hated that she ate exactly one fun-sized Snickers bar every day after dismissal. I hated how she never formatted her documents correctly and couldn't write an all-school memo without also including at least one emoji, gif, or clip art.

I hated Tara Treloff and I prayed for the day when I wouldn't have to see her huge brown eyes glaring at me, sizing me up, seeing through me anymore.

I prayed for that day almost as much as I dreaded it.

Eventually, I rounded the vehicle and settled into the driver's seat. Backing out of the parking space required ignoring a half dozen of Tara's withering side-eyed glances.

After two years of contending with her special brand of assault with deadly glares, I knew not to look her in the eye when she was in moods like this one.

I made it to the interstate before Tara started digging through her tote bag. The thing was big enough to hold a turkey dinner, a litter of kittens, and a baby grand piano. I would experience no surprise if she pulled out a perfectly roasted drumstick and offered it to me.

Tara did crazy things like that. She whipped up six dozen cookies for the staff because she had some extra eggs in the fridge, and made decorative banners for the hallways out of old t-shirts, and invented comparative writing exercises using a random bag of buttons she found in her closet.

It was crazy—and frustrating as hell. The woman didn't believe in focusing on one thing at a time. She listened to audiobooks while setting up laptops for quarterly assessments and cut out lamination while sitting through team lesson planning meetings and alphabetized homework packets during all-school assemblies.

Instead of handing me a turkey leg, she opened a paperback book. Minutes ticked by while she read, humming to herself as she reacted to the events. Quick gasps, little chuckles, quiet sighs and murmurs filled with emotion. She didn't turn a single page without making her feelings about it known.

I was already choking on her vanilla scent but the addition of her infernal noises twisted knots into the base of my neck. I couldn't stop myself from asking, "This is your plan? Reading the whole ride?"

"It's a long book," she replied, wedging her thumb between the pages to hold her place while she showed me the spine. "It's not like we're going to have a civil conversation."

This was her routine. I'd ask a reasonable question and she'd come back with an outrageous comment that required me to dismiss her or offer an equally outrageous response.

I'd started this, of course. I'd turned her first day on the job and all her reasonable questions into a series of outrageous comments. It was only fair she'd continued it. At this point, the reason for my resentment didn't matter. I'd been awful to her, and grown to well and truly hate her. Nothing was changing that.

"What are you reading?" I asked, my words crisp.

She turned the book over and studied the back cover. *"Game of Thrones."*

"Seriously? Why? I can't see you liking that."

"Why not?" she snapped. "You think the only thing I read is *Because of Winn-Dixie* and *The Lightning Thief*?"

Honestly, yes.

I imagined Tara went home to an apartment packed with dog-eared children's books, Play-Doh, Unifix cubes, and a stack of old magazines she kept for collage purposes. I was willing to bet she had a jar of dried macaroni on her coffee table too.

"No, not at all," I lied. "It's just a very violent series. I didn't think you'd be into that."

Tara said things like "crisscross applesauce" and cried during the third grade strings concert and wore gloves embroidered with dog faces.

She took her shoes off whenever she sat at her desk and had a knitted cover for her tissue box.

I couldn't imagine the same person choosing to page through The Red Wedding for pleasure.

"That's funny," she murmured, no humor in her voice.

"Which part?"

"The part where you think you know anything about my preferences," she replied. "I mean, you're taking your tiny teaspoon of knowledge about me and shaking it up with outdated kindergarten teacher stereotypes and churning out some real amusing bullshit."

I stared at the road ahead, allowing miles to pass before speaking again. I hated Tara but it wasn't one-sided. She hated me just as much and there was no way I could forget it.

"I asked, didn't I? If you're determined to believe that I'm the problem here, that's your prerogative, but don't forget I fucking asked. It's a lot more than you've ever done."

"That's because you *are* the problem here," she cried, slapping her book against her leg. I glanced at her long, trouser-clad legs before forcing my gaze back to the road. "But yeah, let's pretend none of that exists and I'll justify my choice of books to you."

When she was alive, my grandmother lived in an old farmhouse. The basement—she'd called it *down cellar* as one did in New England—was dark and creepy. Nightmare-quality creepy.

The worst part was all the small rooms with passageways that opened into more passageways like cobwebbed matryoshka dolls. The lure of exploring those spaces was too much to avoid for any kid and I fell victim time after time. And every damn time, I lost my way inside one of those passages. I'd find myself turned around in the dark, not sure which way I'd come or how to get out, and certain I'd never be found.

That was what arguing with Tara felt like. The reasonable solution was retracing my steps and sliding my hands along the walls until I found an exit, but I always opted for screaming myself hoarse or flailing on the cold dirt floor.

I never took the smart route with her. When we'd first started working together, every conversation was a basement nightmare. It was still a nightmare but now it often came with a side of evil entertainment. She made it really damn entertaining to hate her. She showed up to every fight, took all the bait, and debated everything I dangled in front of her.

I still didn't know how to get out of this space. At least I'd learned how to amuse myself while I flailed and screamed.

"Why am I the problem, Tara? Is it my high expecta-tions for teachers and students? Is it my stellar record in the classroom? Perhaps it's all the parents who thank me for helping them get their kid into an elite high school. Yeah, must be it. That's the root of the problem, me excelling at my job."

From the corner of my eye, I saw her shaking her head. "You're so great," she drawled. "You're just amazing in every way. That's the real issue. You re just overwhelmingly perfect."

"Evidently, you have an issue with that."

She shoved a bookmark between the pages, saying, "I have an issue with you thinking you're always right, with your refusal to consider any other point of view, with your belief the only outcomes that matter are test scores and high school admissions. I have a gigantic problem with you behaving as if I'm ruining your life by *me* excelling at *my* job."

"You're skipping the part where I am often right and it's a waste of time to consider other perspectives," I said. I skipped the part where I acknowledged she *was* ruining my life.

She threw her hands up and glared out the window. "I brought this book so we wouldn't have to talk," she said, her words just above a whisper. "You could drive, I could read, never the two shall interact. I'm trying, Drew, and you're being a psycho. If you're going to tear down my every attempt at making this work, you might as well pull over and let me out because we know how you want this to end and we know you always get your way."

She was wrong about that. She didn't know how I wanted this to end. She thought she knew but she had no idea.

And I didn't always get my way. Not when it mattered the most.

CHAPTER FOUR

TARA

I WOKE up with dread in my belly. I should've been excited about this training but I couldn't get excited about anything when the prospect of unemployment loomed large on my horizon.

There was a difference between aggressively debating meaningful points with Drew and flat-out fighting with him.

Yesterday was a fight and it confirmed all of my suspicions. Drew intended to block me at every turn and, somehow, he was going to get away with it. He always got away with it. I didn't understand what made him so untouchable.

I checked the time on my phone and gathered my things for the day. Thanks to all the tossing and turning, I was awake and ready to go earlier than necessary. At least it gave me time to grab some coffee before the session started in one of the hotel's large meeting spaces.

These events always had coffee and tea available but I loathed coffee brewed in large quantities. I couldn't explain the difference between light and dark roasts if I tried. Nope, I required a make-it-just-for-me coffee.

I couldn't remember whether there was a coffee shop in the hotel lobby. I hadn't paid much attention when we'd arrived last night.

After hours in a confined space with Drew, the only thing I'd cared about was getting away from him. The entire situation was bad enough but after we'd stopped at a sandwich shop for a quick meal, he'd rolled his shirtsleeves up to his elbows and drove the remainder of the distance with bare forearms.

The audacity of that fucker. Really.

But, with respect to coffee, I knew hiking around downtown Albany was a possibility. I shrugged on my coat, hoisted my bag to my shoulder, and headed toward the door. I didn't mind leaving the hotel this morning, considering I'd be closed up in a windowless ballroom for the next eight hours and—

—and I walked straight into Drew freakin' Larsen.

"Oh my god, what are you doing here?" I cried, stumbling back against the door and slapping a hand to my galloping heart.

He responded with a slow blink and a scowl that told me he wasn't concerned with the fact he'd scared ten years off my life by lurking outside my room.

He extended his arm toward me and it was then I realized he was holding two cups of coffee. "Here."

I took the cup and examined the order label on the side. Large almond milk latte with extra cinnamon sprinkle. My exact wintertime order. "What—how—I mean—thank you?"

He shook his head as if my gratitude was annoying. Typical. Leave it to Drew, with his impeccably pressed trousers and dress shirt that fit like skin, to blow off the one pleasant word I said to him. If there was justice in the universe, Drew Larsen wouldn't have made clothes look this good.

"Everything about that order sounds terrible," he said, taking off in the direction of the lobby.

I followed but refused to match his near-sprinting strides. We had plenty of time and I required all of it to figure out how he knew how I took my coffee. "And yet you still ordered it."

"Only because I wasn't going to risk arriving late because you require specialty coffee." Drew glanced over his shoulder and realized I was several paces behind him. He stopped, waited for me to reach him. He raised his paper cup before continuing down the hall. "Black."

"Congratulations," I replied. "Unfortunately, the only prize for drinking bitter, boring coffee is the hollow sense of self-importance. I hope you enjoy it."

"You could've just said thank you," he grumbled.

"I did. It was the first thing I said."

"No, you screamed like I was holding a decapitated head rather than a cup of nausea-inspiring coffee," he replied.

"Perhaps I screamed because you were lurking outside my door and that shit is creepy. You could've knocked or even texted me."

"I was *waiting* for you," he snapped. "I didn't want to bother you."

"Oh, so you'd prefer to give me a heart attack first thing in the morning? How kind of you."

"There is no winning with you," he murmured.

"With *me?* You're out of your damn mind if you think *I'm*—"

Drew edged into my space, his hand hovering over the small of my back but never actually touching me as he shuffled me around a corner.

Completely unamused by this morning's antics, I leaned back against the wall and took a sip of my coffee. Cinnamony perfection. He watched me for a second, so damn perturbed by my refusal to take his bullshit seriously.

With his hand flattened on the wall over my shoulder, he leaned down to meet my gaze, his chest nearly brushing mine. "Say thank you."

I arched a brow. "I already did."

"Say it and mean it."

We stared at each other for a moment, the scents of coffee and cinnamon swirling around us.

We hated each other, that was fact. But there were instances like these where I wondered if I understood the full spectrum of hate.

Maybe there were corners of hate that were more than wanting someone to burst into flames or, less fatally, never be able to find a phone charger when they needed it. More than wanting to beat them at every game.

More than any of that, maybe hate wasn't hate at all.

"Tara," he whispered, edging even closer. At this range, I could see the flecks of gold and amber in his eyes and imagine the texture of his dark, close-cut beard. "Say it."

"Thank you for the coffee." There were ten sarcastic, cutting jabs waiting on my tongue but I held them all back as he watched the words moving over my lips like they had shapes and forms he could distinguish from thin air. "Thank you for remembering what I like."

"You're welcome." He stared at me with those dark eyes of his, as if he could see inside me and page through my thoughts. Except he didn't, he couldn't. I didn't allow it. He saw only what he chose and only the worst of me. "We should go. I don't want to be late."

"We're not going to be late." I glanced at the arm extended toward the wall and then back up at Drew. "But since it's important to you, why don't you back up and return to your body bubble? We're not going to be on time if we stay here all morning."

He closed his eyes, blew out a breath, and jolted away from me like I was toxic waste. He ran his palm over his jaw and marched back to the main corridor without sparing me a second glance.

"Come on," he called, back on his impatient bullshit. "Ten minutes early is the same as five minutes late."

I knocked my head against the wall with a groan. This obnoxious fucker.

CHAPTER FIVE

TARA

TEN MINUTES EARLY, five minutes late—none of it mattered. Not when this conference kicked off with half an hour of pastries and networking—and Drew was acting strange.

He was always strange. Anyone who started sentences with "This might be nihilistic of me, but" qualified as strange. However, this morning had the makings of a personal best for him. Creeping outside my hotel room was a solid start and now, when he could've been mingling with the other participants like an ordinary person, Drew was posted up at the coffee station. That would've been perfectly reasonable if he hadn't waggled his black venti at me in the hallway.

At first, I thought he was simply avoiding me. Hanging out with the dark roast and heavy cream because he wanted to unload another lecture about something he knew and I didn't made sense considering this wasn't the forum for another one of our heated discussions.

But *I'd* left *him* alone.

The second we'd checked in for the training and received badges announcing our names and schools, I'd split to make the most of this interstitial time before the session launched.

There were mini muffins to hoard and people to meet, none of whom were angling to get me fired. In the ten minutes since, Drew had only made it as far as the coffee station and *that* was very strange.

This should've been Drew's jam. He loved being the guy who knew people, the one who had every contact in his phone.

He liked being able to say, "Let me give Thatguy at Thatplace a call. He'll handle this in seventy-one seconds."

From the other side of the ballroom, I watched as Drew went on fussing with sugar packets. Sugar, of all things. He'd die before he sweetened his coffee. He kept it black and bitter, same as his soul.

Okay, that was unfair. His soul wasn't completely black—or bitter. He never let anyone forget his Ivy League pedigree but he also cared about our school and the teachers and students in undeniably massive ways. He went out of his way to celebrate their successes and support their development even if he scowled at my cookies-and-songs approach to celebration.

His soul was only black and bitter when it turned its glare on me, which was really fucking frustrating. I was a ray of goddamn sunshine. Everyone loved me. I brought baked goods to early morning staff meetings and never missed a birthday. I was a good person, dammit. Never before had anyone regarded me with such open, detailed, absurd hostility.

And somehow, I'd spent two years on the receiving end of that hostility without realizing until this morning that Drew Larsen was paralytically shy. I couldn't believe I hadn't noticed it until now but watching him awkward-wiggle through introductions at the coffee station made it painfully obvious.

At this moment, he was pretending to be busy with the milk carafes—*Which kind of milk is that? Half and half, amazing. Is this one full? How about I give it a shake to find out. Oh, yes, very full. Wow. Full of milk this carafe is. So full I'm unable to carry on a conversation. Lots of milk going on here, step aside, please. I must tend to inspecting this milk, thank you*—to avoid the pair of women angling for his attention. They were also eye-fucking him like he was a breakfast treat they intended to share.

Cinnamon roll for two, please.

It was his own fault. It happened every time he wore those charcoal gray trousers with the subtle pinstripe.

I'd caught our seventy-two-year-old school nurse checking him out the last time he'd worn them.

If Drew noticed that kind of attention, he didn't let on. As far as I could tell, the only thing he currently noticed was his desire to avoid the shit out of talking to people.

My arch enemy, the man who seized every opportunity to crow about Dartmouth and being the first person on staff behind Lauren six years ago, was *shy*.

In a way, it made sense that I'd never noticed. Drew knew the entire staff the way I knew my siblings, and he was on a first name basis with every student's parents. Whenever new people visited our school, he entered those situations in a position of clear, comfortable authority. Giving tours and answering questions about our academic program wasn't the same kind of interaction as meeting brand-new people at an out-of-town conference.

Suddenly, I saw his thirst to rub his fancy Dartmouth degree in my face less as a personal attack and more of a self-defense mechanism.

It was still a personal attack but now the origin made more sense. It wasn't about me, not all the way.

The King of Dartmouth was a little insecure and he covered it up by being a colossal asshole.

Funny how that worked out sometimes.

For no reason other than curiosity—only curiosity, not some odd desire to rescue him from another ten minutes of unstructured mingling and dairy analysis— I excused myself from the group of academic leaders from a network of independent schools and made my way toward him.

When I reached the coffee station, I sidled up beside him and set my cup down. I popped the lid and added an unnecessary shake of cinnamon.

He glanced over, staring at my cup while he circled a stirring stick around his. "Why? Just...why do you pervert a perfectly good beverage with powdered cinnamon?"

"Because it's fun," I replied, my gaze locked on the cup. "A little unexpected too."

"A pickle would be unexpected," he remarked "Cinnamon is just a poor choice."

I glanced at the packet of sugar clutched in his hand. I wanted to tease him about it—about everything—but more than that, I wanted to make this work between us.

I wanted to stop meeting him at his level with all the taunts and harsh criticisms and one-ups.

I wanted to channel my energy into decorating my

little apartment for Christmas and thinking up the perfect gifts for my friends and family rather than updating my résumé.

I wanted to go back to being me, that goddamn ray of sunshine I was, not the angry, competitive brat I turned into around him.

A ray of sunshine would stay here, right beside the storm cloud until his thunder dissipated. I could do that for him. I could get him through this—and maybe then we'd be able to get through this career quicksand together because it wouldn't be *Drew is the best* and *Tara is the worst* anymore.

The rivalry would die and I'd finally banish the image of me grabbing him by the beard and ordering him to kneel and—well, the specifics of those errant fantasies were irrelevant.

Aside from the beard-grabbing and such, we'd be a team, sunshine and storm clouds all the way, and I'd like that. Instead of fighting over everything, we'd be able to lean on each other in ways that had nothing to do with one-upmanship or competency signaling.

If we were a team, I wouldn't hate it when he scheduled parent-teacher conferences for my grade levels and he wouldn't grouse about me developing fun instructional skits with his teachers. We'd take all the energy we'd devoted to fighting this war and put it toward our partnership.

"I was looking over the session topics for today and tomorrow," I started, finally glancing up at him, 'and I have some ideas."

"It's always a treat when you think for yourself, Miss Treloff."

Not taking the bait. Not taking the bait. Not taking the —"I was thinking about how to share out this content with the staff. Since we have a few minutes now, maybe we could brainstorm some plans for disseminating information. We don't have a lot of time to play with in terms of whole staff meetings but there is a good deal of flexibility with our grade team meetings and common planning time. I'm also seeing a lot of overlap in content that would be helpful for a few of my folks and a few of yours. We could—"

"I've already developed dissemination plans," he interrupted, tossing the sugar back in the bin. "I'll send you my drafts. Just use that and save yourself the mental workout. You're here to listen and learn. Don't make it more complicated on yourself, Tara."

He turned, stalked back to the table with his coffee, and taught me the most valuable lesson of the day: never give Drew Larsen the benefit of the doubt again.

He didn't need it and he sure as hell didn't deserve it.

CHAPTER SIX

TARA

WE SAT side by side in our assigned seats but acted as if we didn't know each other. Every time the session called for participants to pair up or engage in an exercise, Drew and I turned in opposite directions.

We ignored the shit out of each other. It was better than fighting but it left me with the overwhelming sense that my time would be better utilized searching for a new job.

I could barely concentrate on the information being presented. The speaker was masterful and I was eager to share the content with my team, though I couldn't get away from the reality I might not have a team for much longer.

By the time late afternoon rolled around and the session was nearing its close for the day, I was ready to faceplant on the bed in my hotel room and forget about Drew, even for five minutes.

For all that I wanted the faceplant and the forgetting, the collaborative thing to do next would be debriefing the training over dinner as Lauren had instructed.

And as much as I hated to admit it, if Drew and I couldn't manage to talk shop over dinner, we had no business working together. And it wasn't like I wanted to walk across the hotel parking lot and request a table for one at Outback Steakhouse.

With my luck, Drew would have the same plan and we'd wind up lumped together in the Lonely, Party of One section.

We'd ignore each other, of course.

During a short break, the event's lead trainer Doug moved to the front of the room, his phone and a sheaf of papers clutched in one hand. He raised the other hand, gathering the attention of the participants.

"We hate to announce this because we're loving the time we've spent with you today and we're really looking forward to tomorrow's session," he said. "However, we just got word the airport will be closing at nine o'clock tonight in preparation for an incoming blizzard. It looks like the winter storm coming up from the south started moving faster than the weather folks expected while some cold air dipping down from the

Arctic has stalled near the Lakes Region. All this has combined into an unexpected beast of a storm and we're right in the middle of it."

As the room erupted in a low panic—as much as any bunch of educators allowed themselves to erupt into any degree of panic—I turned to my right but found Drew's seat empty.

This was the product of ignoring someone so hard, you actually blacked out their existence. I swiveled in my seat, glancing toward the coffee station that'd held his interest during all the other breaks today. He wasn't there. I scanned the room but couldn't spot him.

The mean, petty part of my mind, the part that only roared to life when Drew was involved, had me wondering whether he'd left without me.

He hated me and resented me, and he wanted me fired. But I wasn't sure whether he'd abandon me in Albany, New York during a blizzard.

Underneath the insults and hostility, he remembered my coffee order and hung around my door like a proper stalker to deliver it.

"And he's an obnoxious fucker who will stop at nothing to get rid of me," I muttered to myself as I slipped my phone from my pocket. "Should've learned that lesson a long, long time ago."

I started tapping out a message to him when I heard his voice behind me.

"Come on," he said, his hand on the back of my chair. His knuckles brushed my shoulder. "If we hit the road now, we'll beat the storm."

I glanced up at him. "Beat it, how?"

He rolled his eyes. "We will arrive in Boston before the storm. Understand? Or do I need to give you a meteorology lesson? Surely they covered the basics at Bridgewater State."

That fucker. He really needed to get some new material. The "Tara went to a lame ass state school" routine was old and boring. If he wanted some juicy content, he need only turn to my love of avocado toast, the houseplants I considered my babies, all the meditation apps I subscribed to, and my complete inability to stop buying things from Instagram.

"Don't you think it would be better to wait until tomorrow morning?" I asked. "I mean, they're closing the airport because of this. I don't have a Dartmouth education in meteorology to back me up here but I did grow up outside Worcester and have a weather app on my phone, and I know that shit doesn't happen often."

"Tomorrow morning," he repeated as if I'd suggested we simply chop up some Snickers bars and turn the blizzard into Dairy Queen Blizzards. "I bet that makes sense to you but no, I don't think it would be better. The roads will be a disaster. If we leave now, we'll be home before a single flurry hits the ground."

I glanced back at Doug and the people congregated around him. "Why would they send everyone home and cancel tomorrow's session if it isn't going to snow for hours?"

He huffed, sighed, rolled his eyes. And his knuckles grazed my shoulder—once, twice, three times. Squeezed his eyes shut and exhaled like I'd punched the air out of him. This guy was seriously impatient.

"Because it's a handful of days before Christmas and they don't want anyone stranded here. They want everyone to get out while they can, Tara, and I can't say I blame them. We all have somewhere to be and someone wanting to be with us for the holiday. Someone we want to be with more than anything, right?" I blinked up at him as he brushed my shoulder once more. "Get your things. I'll check us out and meet you in the lobby."

I stared after Drew while he marched through the ballroom. Now, I was left with one final car ride to broker a peace deal. As I watched those charcoal gray trousers and that tight ass striding out of sight, I couldn't see how to pull this off.

CHAPTER SEVEN

DREW

I WASN'T good at admitting my mistakes.

If I could get by without acknowledging missteps and miscalculations, I did. I didn't enjoy being wrong and I enjoyed announcing those rare moments even less. It wasn't my finest quality but at least I possessed enough awareness to keep from making many mistakes in the first place.

Today was the great exception to all of those rules. I was racking up mistakes like my life was a hot game of Skee-Ball. Any minute now, I'd have to admit I was wrong.

My greatest miscalculation of the day involved my ability to drive through a white-out blizzard. Yes, the same blizzard I'd argued I could outrun. Hell, I grew up in western Pennsylvania and went to college in northern New Hampshire. I knew all there was about driving in snow.

This wasn't snow.

This was an avalanche. I was only half certain I was driving on a road rather than eight feet of packed powder. Hell, it was possible I wasn't even driving. For all I could tell, the storm was steering.

We should've been out of the mountains by now. We should've been through the worst of this weather. We should've and I would've been able to confirm that if my GPS signal stayed stable long enough to give me an update on our location.

For the nineteenth time since hitting the interstate outside of Albany four hours ago, Tara asked, "Are you sure about this?"

This time, I didn't snap back at her. For as much as I couldn't deal with her and her big, dark eyes and the subtle scent of vanilla that surrounded her, I was too exhausted from white-knuckling it through this snow globe. I was too worried we'd end up spending the night together in my car. Too drained from everything between us. I couldn't do it. I couldn't be the villain in her story right now.

"If you see an alternative, Tara, please share it with me."

Before she could answer, red lights flashed in my

rearview mirror. A siren cut through the howling wind. Of fucking course.

"Maybe they've arrived with your alternative," she muttered as I made my way to the shoulder of the highway. Or, what I believed to be the shoulder. Lane lines had disappeared hours ago.

You knew it was a bad storm when the patrolman pulled up alongside you rather than climbing out of his vehicle.

When I edged the window down, he boomed, "Sir, you need to get off this road for your safety and the safety of emergency responders. The interstates are closing within the hour."

"Okay, but"—I glanced at the road—"where are we?"

The blowing snow made it impossible to know for sure, but it seemed like the patrolman rolled his eyes at me. "I'll escort you to the next exit."

Without a word to Tara, I followed the cruiser's flashing lights for several minutes. Not even the road signs helped place our location as they were caked with wind-whipped snow and ice.

At the end of the off ramp, I swung my gaze from left to right. I didn't know where we were but I was positive this wasn't metro Boston. No, we were still in the Berkshires, which meant we'd traveled a fraction of the distance in all this time.

"Do you see that sign? Over there?" Tara asked, leaning into my space to point out my window. Like I needed that right now. "It looks like it says something about an inn. That direction."

When we'd left Albany, I'd had a simple plan: get the fuck home. Drop off the bane of my existence, sell my car, and then bathe in boiling acid until I'd scrubbed the memory of vanilla from my skin.

Simple plan, easy to execute. No blizzard was stopping me.

But here I was, with Tara's elbow jutting into my chest and her hair swishing against my chin as she gestured toward the only legible sign for a hundred miles, and it promised an inn five miles ahead.

It was an alternative but god help me, I couldn't survive another night with a wall between us.

I couldn't do it. There was no way. Not when I'd know she was freeing her hair from the afternoon's bun, undressing, showering, slipping between the sheets on the other side of that wall.

Not when she was *right there.*

"Drew, come *on.*" She pulled back her arm, settled in her seat. *Thank god.* "What else are we going to do? Where are we going to go? It's late and it's dark and the only snacks we have are the cookies I nabbed from the training. I am hungry and tired, and I'm so cold, and I think—"

"Why are you cold?" Not thinking for a damn second, I reached over and gathered her hands between mine. She was *freezing*, her fingers like icicles. And she felt—no, I wasn't going there. Couldn't. It didn't matter how her skin felt against mine. Didn't fucking matter. "You should've said something," I growled.

That's right. It's her fault. Keep leaning into that strategy. It hasn't failed me yet.

"I'm okay," she said, rubbing her palms together as I held her.

Oh, Jesus Christ, I'm still holding her hands. I'm holding her hands and she's letting me and the universe hasn't imploded. But I had to stop, this *had* to stop.

"Fine, we'll see about this inn." I set her hands in her lap, which granted me the misery of brushing my knuckles over her thighs.

Shouldn't have done that. No. Should *not* have done that.

I stabbed some buttons on the center console, flipping on the seat warmers and cranking the heat. I'd kept it cooler to prevent the windows from fogging and hadn't noticed the cold, mostly because I spent the past few hours panic sweating as I struggled to keep us from spinning out and t-boning a guardrail.

With a curse under my breath, I turned left toward the inn. These roads were as bad as the highway but a long stone wall bracketed either side, forming a makeshift trail. The minutes crawled by as I itched to take her hands in mine again, to keep her warm.

Eventually, we turned down the inn's long, winding driveway. I prayed for two rooms on opposite ends of the property. I required acreage between us because there was no way I could endure another night like the last. It had been brutal.

The amount of time I'd spent sitting on my bed, still and steady and just fucking listening for any sound of her was...well, it was embarrassing. I was tired in a way that my eyes seemed incapable of closing for more than a blink, my muscles wrought too tight to loosen enough to rest.

And—and she was cold. She was cold and I couldn't reach over to warm her because we opposed each other like magnetic poles. The order and function of the planet would have to collapse before we could do anything but dance around each other because we weren't nearly as different as I wanted to believe.

No, Tara Treloff and I were exactly the same and I couldn't handle that at all.

"This place doesn't look too..." Her voice trailed off.

"Inhabited?" I murmured, rolling to a stop at the entrance. As best I could tell through the snow, a series of small cottages were stringed along either side of the main house, the only building with lights illuminated. "Let's just go up to the door and see if there's—"

"Room at the inn?" she asked, laughing. "Jesus, I hope so."

"That's not even funny," I said, but I couldn't help but laugh along with her. Because I enjoyed torturing myself, I reached for the hands she clasped in her lap. She felt like a barely defrosted ribeye. "Any better?"

She wiggled her shoulders in that obscenely cute way of hers. She always did that when she didn't want to be a problem.

Be my problem, sweetheart.

"I'll be better when I have some hot chocolate and Kahlua and fifteen blankets," she said, giving my fingers a curious glance as I rubbed the back of her hand. "Which is why we need to get in there before we're sent off to the barn. I'm a bit rusty on my catechism but I don't believe the wise men brought Kahlua. They should've. Gold, frankincense, and Kahlua sounds more useful. Even vodka would've been better than myrrh. Right? Who the hell needs myrrh?"

I reached into the backseat for my coat and shrugged it on. "I don't know, Tara."

"You're—wait a second. You're admitting you don't *know* something?"

The squeal in her voice informed me I'd just fallen into a trap of my own making. *Brilliant.* 'Can we reserve the discussion of my general fallibility for another day? When your lips aren't turning blue and we're not in danger of being snowed inside the car?"

Tara gave a groan of indignance—I knew this because I'd categorized her groans and replayed them on a loop every time I wanted to resent something for existing while also protecting it with my life—and pushed the door open. Snow gusted in and she shrieked at it as if that would help.

"Fuck my life," I mumbled as I rounded the car to shield her from the worst of the storm. "Take that hat off. It's going to trap water on your head. Take mine."

"What? No. Let's just do this," she replied, trudging through the drifts.

I caught up with her quickly and more a result of wind pushing us together than any plan of mine, we huddled close to each other as we climbed the front steps and rang the bell.

It was miserably cold and it didn't matter how many blizzards I lived through, the churning roar of it always surprised me. It was the wind that made these storms treacherous, not the snow, not even the cold. It was always the things you couldn't see that changed everything.

We waited, our heads ducked low and our arms folded tight to our bodies.

And we waited.

And we waited some more. That I didn't sweep her into my arms or press her hands under my shirt when I heard her teeth chattering was a major accomplishment not unlike hiking the Atacama or swimming the English Channel or me leaving one of her verbal jabs unaddressed.

Finally, several lights flipped on and the door swung open to reveal a woman in a floor-length robe that zipped up to her throat. She beckoned us inside with frantic waves, standing away from the door as we shook off the snow that'd accumulated in the minutes we'd been outside.

"We're so sorry to bother you but the interstate is closed and we're kind of stranded," Tara said. "Is there any chance you have two rooms available?"

Immediately, the woman replied with a bewildered, "No."

"Oh. Okay," Tara said. "I guess we'll have to f-f-f-ind somewhere else." She glanced over at me. "For the first time in my life, I really sympathize with Mary."

"We're only open in the summer, you see," the woman continued. "We're closed up for the winter. We turn off the water to the units before the first frost and keep the heat in the low sixties to prevent the pipes from bursting. We only keep one unit functional this time of year in case my sister-in-law comes up from—"

"We'll take it," I said, despite the absolute horror of this proposition.

The roads were horrendous and only getting worse, and it was too late to go looking for substitutes. I'd manage. I didn't have any choice. I'd post up on a couch or chair. A bathtub, if need be. The floor would do in a pinch. I'd manage.

I'd managed for two years, hadn't I? I could make it through one night even if it crushed my soul and ate what remained of my spirit with a spoon.

"It's a one-bedroom and it's not in any condition for guests," she argued. "We're in the middle of a remodel. The furniture is piled up in the center of the room, the wallpaper has been scraped off, the bathroom is halfway painted—"

"We will take it," I repeated.

"Honestly, it's fine," Tara said through her shivers. I was going to die if that didn't stop soon. "We don't mind."

The woman twisted her fingers together as she glanced between us. "At least let me give you some supper. I have a bit of shepherd's pie leftover if that suits you."

"We'd love that. You're extremely kind and generous," Tara said. "Thank you."

The woman shuffled down the hall, quickly returning with a grocery tote and a key hanging from a chunk of worn wood. Tara reached out with shaking hands but I snatched up both items.

"I have this," I murmured to her as we turned toward the door. "Concentrate your efforts on not turning into a popsicle, okay? The last thing I need right now is you losing a couple of toes to hypothermia."

"Yeah, Drew, I'm doing this to annoy you."

Once we were outside again, I pointed at my SUV, saying, "I'll grab the bags, you head toward the cottage." This meant I had to hand over the key which only made me grabbing for it more egregious as far as my bad behavior was concerned. "Go on. Let yourself in since your goal is not, despite every indication to the contrary, to drive me mad. I'll be right behind you."

In a simpler world, Tara would've trudged through the knee-deep snow and unlocked the door to the space we were sharing tonight without incident.

Unfortunately for me, I didn't live in a simple world.

I lived in a world where I wanted my colleague so much, I plowed all the way through lust and came out the other side in the deep end of resentment.

And Tara lived in a world where those useless boots of hers sent her sliding on a patch of ice and tumbling face first into a snow drift.

I jogged toward her, careful for the ice, and scooped

her out of the snow. "What the fuck was that, Treloff?" I shouted, hoisting her over my shoulder. It was a good thing she was doll-sized. I wouldn't have been able to manage Tara, the luggage, and the shepherd's pie otherwise and fuck me if I was leaving the shepherd's pie behind.

"I fell in the snow, Drew."

I rolled my eyes. It saved me from thinking about my cheek and how it was resting on her thigh. "Those boots are useless. No traction whatsoever."

"I'm sure you have a story about how you did something important with snow and boots with extra traction while at Dartmouth," she said, her hands fisting around the back of my coat.

"What the fuck does that mean?" I shouted.

"Just that you always have a story about the amazing things you did at Dartmouth," she replied. "Is there a quota? Like, you have to mention your alma mater three times per day or they'll revoke your preppy boy card? Or are you worried I'll forget? Contrary to your peculiar opinion, people who attended state schools do have long-term memory. I won't forget, Drew."

Snow and ice bit at the side of my face as I pushed the key into the lock. After some jiggling and twisting, the door creaked open. As promised, the space was a wreck but it was dry and relatively warm.

I kicked the door shut and dropped the bags. "You better not fall over when I put you down."

She released her hold on my coat. "I won't."

"I'm not picking you up if you do." I was absolutely picking her up. Anywhere, anytime.

"I'm not asking you to pick me up. You didn't have to pick me up back there. I would've been fine, you know."

"You say that..." With my hands on her waist to guide her, I bent to set her on her feet.

She leaned back against the door, her face stung red from the cold. "And I meant it. I know you think I'm completely incapable but I do know how to get up when I fall down, Drew."

Tara stared up at me, her dark eyes wide and her lips parted, and a violent shiver rattled through her. It killed me to see her like this.

I could fix everything else for her—I could deal with the protocols and scheduling issues she loathed and unjam the copier and anything else that gave her trouble at work—but I couldn't stand here, helpless to do anything but watch while she shook with cold.

"You're the one," she continued, "who thinks it's necessary to rush in and toss people over your shoulder because you think it's your place to instruct them on how to live. Maybe if you offered people a hand when they fell in the snow rather than carrying them through a blizzard and taking away their ability to do anything at all, you'd understand the difference."

A growl rattled in my throat. "Is that how you see it? That I don't understand the *difference*?"

"I don't think you want to understand."

I pivoted, paced the length of the room without concern for my snow-caked trousers or the disarray of furniture. I barely noticed and I didn't care because Tara thought—she actually thought I wanted to fold her into smaller and smaller pieces until she was barely anything at all, like a note passed between seventh graders.

Fuck my life.

Just...fuck my life.

Why did it have to be this way? Why did we have to exist on the same side of the coin yet stand diametrically opposed at all turns? Why couldn't we see each other without the fog of war hanging heavy between us?

I didn't know and I wasn't certain I could keep doing it. This hurt. Every single day, it *hurt*.

When I watched her fingers slide through her hair as she twisted up a bun, I ached to bat her hands away and curl those strands around my fist.

When she took off her shoes, I had to sit on my hands to keep from dragging her feet into my lap.

When she doused teachers with her special blend of

optimism and enthusiasm and get-it-done, my jealous heart hammered against my ribs hard enough to make me gasp.

This fucking hurt.

And now, with her wet and cold and angry because she didn't want me plucking her out of snowbanks, each moment stung like a sucker punch.

I couldn't bear it.

I couldn't stand this, not any longer. I couldn't protect myself by simply hating her because it wasn't enough. If anything, I'd traveled the circumference of hate and built an uncomfortable home for myself on the antagonistic asshole edge of love.

I couldn't tell her that. For as much as I wanted to tell her everything, I couldn't tell her anything. Because I did, I loved her. But it was too tied up with resentment and denial and a firewall of hostility to be the kind of love anyone shared.

I shook my head as the icy wet of my clothes finally registered alongside all the other miseries in my life. "I understand more than you think."

"Oh, really?" she challenged. "Let's hear it, Drew. Come on. Explain to me why you think it's necessary to hobble me at every turn. Explain why it always has to be your way, why I'm always wrong, why I'm never good enough for you, why—"

"Not good enough?" I interrupted. "That's what you think, Tara?"

She pressed her palms to her face, muttering, "Oh my god." Then, "You literally remind me every single day that my expectations aren't high enough for teachers and students." She flung her arms out, sending snow and water flying off her coat. "You criticize my education every chance you get. You tell me, in every manner you can find, that I am not good enough. So, yes, Drew. That's what I think."

Yeah, I really didn't know how to admit—or recover from—my mistakes. That was one of the many side effects of being an academically gifted kid.

Around the time your math teacher started using your exam as the answer key, your ability to believe you might not have all the answers eroded away. It also meant you grew into an adult suffocating under the weight of your own perfectionism and fear of not being good enough.

"I mean—Tara, please—just try to understand—it's not, that's not—" Because words were entirely useless and it seemed I might actually crack in half if I didn't, I reached for her, my hands cupping her cheeks, and I pressed my lips to hers.

For a second, she didn't react. And in that second, I was convinced she was going to toss me into one of those snow drifts.

But then, she curled her hands around the front of my coat. When she didn't knee me in the balls or take a swipe at my jugular, I accepted that as an invitation to flatten her against that door.

It was mad to imagine but maybe we didn't truly hate each other. Maybe we were both camped on the fringes of love and hate—at least sexual chemistry and hate—and waiting for the other to fire the first shot.

Was that it? Was it even possible? That we'd spent all this time circling each other, tormenting each other, spiking barbs at each other—when we really wanted to tear each other apart in bed?

When I was wrong, I was really fucking wrong.

I plucked the beanie from her head and unzipped her coat, all while treating myself to the sweetness of her kisses. I didn't grant myself a moment to consider what I was doing or how it was certain to wreck my life in the process.

I just wanted this minute where we weren't trying to kill each other and I had the good fortune of touching her. I'd deal with everything else later. If I could have this right now, everything else could wait until later.

I shoved my hands under her sweater, groaning into her mouth at the joy of bare—but alarmingly cold —skin. "You need to get warm," I said. "Let me do that for you, baby."

"I'm not your baby," she whispered, her fingers busy opening my coat and peeling it down my arms.

"Right now, you are."

"Not if I say no," she replied.

That stopped everything. I put more space between us than my body appreciated and flattened my hands on the door over her shoulders.

Staring down at her, I asked, "Is that what you want? To say no?"

She glanced up at me, her teeth sunk into her bottom lip. "I'm not your baby."

"Okay." I nodded but maintained the breath of distance between us. "What else?"

Tara stabbed a finger at the room. "If you want me—"

"That is not a question," I murmured with a pointed glance at the tent in my trousers.

"—then you need to earn me."

"You're talking to a classic overachiever. You better believe I can earn you." I hooked my arm under her ass and carried her across the room. The bed sat at a haphazard angle in the center of the room, but there was nothing I cared about less than its location. The only thing that mattered was getting on it—and staying there. "I'm going to get you so hot, I'll be able to lick sweat off your skin."

"That is revolting," she said as I pried her boots off

and chucked them over my shoulder. Those goddamn boots. "Never once in life has that been sexy."

"And yet you'll enjoy it when I do it." I crawled up her body, yanking the blankets out from under her as I went and cocooning us under them. I dropped my weight onto her and found her lips again. "You'll let me do that, Tara. You'll let me and you'll love it."

CHAPTER EIGHT

TARA

"YOU'LL LET me do that, Tara. You'll let me and you'll love it."

Such a Drew thing to say. He didn't even bother asking the question. Once again, he'd decided how it was going to be and issued the memo announcing it without bothering to consult me.

Oh, and I was on my way to naked while he made those decisions—and Drew Larsen was the one actively involved in getting me naked. How the pinstriped fuck did that happen?

As best I could recall, there was my graceful dive into the snowbank followed by a rant about Drew's great big bossy boss tendencies and all of that was capped off with a kiss that rendered everything else in the world irrelevant.

There were his lips, his tongue, his beard, his hands

—and I wasn't worried about my job, wasn't busy loathing him, wasn't even frigid and soggy anymore.

I was a woman-shaped throb of desire and Drew promised to fulfill those desires for me. All I had to do was figure out what I wanted—and let *him* give it to me.

It was more than consent, it was more than the sex, the orgasm, the intimacy of it all. It was accepting that kiss he gave me, the one that knocked all sense and reason from my head, served as a time-out, a truce.

I just didn't know if I could accept this cease-fire after he'd made my life a living hell for *years*. We hadn't been rivals for this trip or the past month—it'd been months and months and months of snapping and snarling and cutting each other down.

Could a kiss really wash it all away? Was I *willing* to let a kiss wash it away?

"Say yes," he whispered to my neck. "Please, Tara."

Part of me knew this was a terrible idea. Another part of me knew it was the only idea.

"Maybe," I conceded, my lips pressed to the sharp line of his bearded jaw. "But don't get any ideas about bossing me around. Don't think you're going to explain any of this to me. In fact, I'm going to fuck the arrogant bastard out of you."

He reached between us, flipped open the buttons at

my waist, and yanked my pants down. "Seems like a big goal, Miss Treloff. You sure you're up for it?"

"So. Fucking. Arrogant." Those words were barely over my tongue when he fisted my panties and ripped them down the middle.

He didn't deserve the triumph of the desperate gasp that move garnered and when his hand slipped between my legs, I couldn't stop the next gasp.

"You don't always have to fight me." He pushed two fingers inside me and we groaned in unison when his thumb met my clit. "You could just shut up and let me destroy you, Tara."

Never had anyone spoken to me the way Drew did —in *and* out of bed.

"Yeah, I could let you do all the work," I said as the sounds of his belt unlatching and his fly unzipping buzzed over my skin. "But we both know you only concern yourself with your needs when you do that."

He leveled me with a glare before pulling my sweater over my head and tossing it aside. My bra followed, then his shirt. There was nothing left between us—nothing but some low-simmering animosity.

"You're so fucking wrong," he whispered as he lowered his lips to my nipple. He gave me two teasing licks and then a bite that felt like a brand. He stroked his cock over my folds, his breath shuddering on my breast. He leaned into me, his throbbing length right up against my opening, and said, "I'm gonna show you how wrong you are."

"This isn't one of those situations where you need to narrate everything, Drew," I said as his thumb worked my clit hard. "I understand you like the sound of your voice but—" Holy fuck, the head of his cock was so thick. Ridiculously thick. Abnormally thick. That wasn't his dick. It had to be his arm, a knee, maybe a tree trunk. "*Ohmygod.*"

He bit my nipple again, chuckling. "What were you saying?"

That fucker.

"That you're spending an unusual amount of time talking."

He gazed at me for a hot, heavy minute as he stroked his cock at my entrance. "Tell me right now if I need to get up and tear my bag apart to find a condom."

"Prepared, are you? Did you expect to get laid at this conference?"

He rolled his eyes toward the ceiling. "No, Tara, I did not expect to get laid at this conference," he replied, condescending as ever.

Why did I feel a laugh bubbling up in response rather than my usual annoyance? Why couldn't I be irritated instead of mildly charmed? "So, you always have condoms with you?"

A growl snapped out of him as he continued stroking himself. "It's just something I have on hand in my travel gear, like a stain remover pen and Band-Aids. Is that all right with you?"

He tapped his erection on my clit and yeah, I wasn't above begging to end this debate and feel that monster inside me. "Tell me if you've been tested recently."

"I have." He bit the other nipple and everything inside me became simultaneously much tighter and much looser. "All clear."

"No condom," I said, even if it wasn't my best moment.

I was on birth control and up-to-date with testing but insisting on condoms was Single Girl 101. I knew better but I just didn't want to let him go—and that realization was even more complicated than the ones involved with kissing him or getting undressed.

He glanced down at me, his brows pinched together and his lips in a firm line. "That would be amazing but are you sure? You're comfortable with that?"

Drew Larsen was a lot of things and I'd bemoaned all of them. Now it seemed I had to add *respectful and considerate in bed* to the list.

Goddamn, this guy. It would've been so much

easier to hate him if he was an across-the-board asshole.

"I am and if you don't mind, I'd like to get started on fucking the arrogance out of you," I replied.

Drew's lips curled up in a sunrise smile. "I'm quite confident this will only make the situation worse."

I reached up, raked my fingers through his beard. "We'll see about that."

His hips snapped forward the second those words passed my lips and the bed creaked beneath us as he pushed into me.

He was so much larger than I expected, and my mind tuned out everything but the heat pumping through my body. He was breaking me down, thrust by thrust, and I wanted to break him too.

"God, baby. You feel—*fuuuuck*."

"Not your baby."

I couldn't do that, not even while his cock hit spots that made me cross-eyed and it was likely I was drooling all over myself, and I'd probably have a pronounced limp tomorrow.

I could fuck him and I could enjoy this night and I could figure out how to go deal with this mess tomorrow but I couldn't be his baby.

"Please, fuck, Tara," he groaned. He sounded almost…sorrowful and broken. As if my refusal to give him every last corner of me was hurting *him*. But that couldn't be right. "Please stop fucking fighting me."

I wanted to protest, to explain that we fought as a matter of course, but that would have required me to speak words. I was capable of moans and babble, and nothing more.

And I didn't think I could handle it, not when it was possible I was breaking down with him.

He continued slamming into me, panting and gasping and growling, and whispered, "Just let me give this to you." I nodded, too lost to form words, and his teeth scraped over my neck. "Is it possible to worship someone and wreck them at the same time? Do you feel that?"

I nodded again, and he growled as he pumped into me. His fingers moved to my clit and this was what he meant by wrecking me. There was no way I could live through this. These sensations—his cock, his fingers, his lips, his roared release—they took me under.

As if he knew I needed something to keep me from falling apart, Drew tangled his arms around me and held me while I gasped and shook. He stayed inside me, pulsing and throbbing and making me wonder whether my skin was actual fire, and he marked my chest and neck and mouth with kisses.

Minutes passed before the stars faded from behind my eyes and reality pushed to the front of my mind.

"What did we just do?" I whispered.

"I don't know," he murmured against my neck. "But I want to do it again."

"Yeah." I could've argued this point. Could've told him it was a one and done situation. But that would've been extremely silly because we were naked and stuck here for at least twelve hours more. To think we'd pass that time without making good use of this bed was hilarious. "I didn't expect quite so…*much* from you. Your cock is, like, insane."

He lifted his head, his lips tipped up in a half smile. "In a complimentary way?"

"Maybe," I hedged. "I'm not positive but I think some of my internal organs have been relocated to accommodate all that, ah, insanity of yours."

Drew skimmed a hand down my torso, stopping below my belly button. "That's fair since your pussy melted a significant portion of my brain. I've blacked out all of logical positivism."

"That's fine," I replied. "You didn't need it and you won't miss it. I, on the other hand, probably need to retrieve my organs. Or something like that."

Nodding, he dragged his fingers over my tummy in swirls and circles that sent hot tingles through my body. "That does seem like a priority." When I murmured in agreement, he continued, "Have you warmed up?"

I gripped his wrist, flattening his hand on my skin. "How do I feel?"

Without blinking, he rumbled, "Hot as fuck."

There was no stopping the blush that reddened my cheeks. "Does that answer your question?"

"It's cute how you're fishing for compliments now." He rubbed his knuckles over his beard. "And you call me arrogant."

"That's because you are," I said with a laugh.

"Is that all I am? Arrogant?"

I gave him an impatient frown. "Didn't I *just* say nice things about your dick? Like, really nice things? And didn't I *just* enjoy that same dick in a very major way?"

"So…I'm an arrogant dick to you?"

I laughed. "Oftentimes, yes." I thought back to the coffee station. "If there's some other side I'm missing, this is your chance to show me."

He considered this for a moment, nodding his head in tiny, tiny bobs and moving his fingers over my skin. Then, "You are—you're so fucking beautiful, Tara. And my god, your pussy is the best place I've ever visited."

"If you're good, I'll let you lick it."

CHAPTER NINE

DREW

THERE WERE many problems with blizzards.

They always resulted in power outages and property damage. They shut down highways and stranded people at hole-in-the-wall inns. And, for a time, they slowed life to a standstill.

Everyone stayed huddled inside and the world as we knew it stopped for a moment. Even Dunkin Donuts shut down during the worst storms.

But the storm always cleared. Blindingly bright sun reflected off sparkling snowbanks and filled the space once held by low, dense clouds, and life started up again. If the hum of a snow blower in the distance wasn't adequate proof, the fact Tara had rolled away from me in the night and huddled up to the edge of the bed, the blankets tucked around her like a burrito, did the trick.

The only way for me to survive after this colossal misstep was leaving the school. I couldn't envision my world without Bayside. That place was my life but it wasn't about the job. It was the people, the community, the purpose. It was my place and yeah, I was a bit feral when it came to protecting it. I didn't know how I could ever leave.

But we'd crossed some serious lines in the past few hours. If I thought it was difficult to share an office with Princess Rainbow Sparkle before wearing her thighs as ear muffs, the cloud of vanilla was the least of my problems now.

Unfortunately, I had a long road of suffering between now and June as I wasn't about to ditch my teachers and students midyear. I was all for dick moves —clearly—but that wasn't one I was making.

I stared at her dark hair fanned out on the pillow. I ran my fingers through the strands one more time. "Tara," I said, not at all softly, "we need to get going."

She shifted in her blanket burrito, her chin tucked against her shoulder as she regarded me with slow, sleepy blinks. And then—*fuuuuuuuuck me*—she smiled the dirtiest little grin in the world, saying, "After last night, that is not how I expected you to wake me up."

I yanked at the covers, unraveling them, and dragged her back to the middle of the bed. I wasn't thinking about the ramifications of her comment.

We had a long drive back to Boston to be distant and awkward and whatever we were to each other now.

"Then you shouldn't have barricaded yourself."

She wrapped her arms around my torso. "That's how I sleep."

I settled between her legs. "It's the wrong way to sleep."

She hooked her legs around my waist. "For fuck's sake, Drew. It's not up for debate."

I pushed inside her and we groaned in unison. "Maybe it is when you're sleeping with me."

She drove her heel into my ass cheek. "Maybe you should give it a try. You might like it."

I rested my forehead on the valley between her breasts. She was delicious here. And everywhere else. "I guarantee you I'm not going to like being swaddled up beside you."

She ran her short nails up my back. "I didn't say anything about being *beside* me. Swaddle *with* me. If you were as smart as you claim, you would've done that from the start. Instead of all this reorganization, you could've fucked me from behind. We'd be having warm, lazy spoon sex rather than slightly chilly, energetic sex. Just so you know, I'm all about the lazy morning spoon sex."

I gathered the blankets tight around us and scooped

a hand under her ass to keep her even closer. "Let's test this hypothesis by trying both."

"HEY, SO..." she started, shooting me a sidelong glance as our bodies cooled, "my family does a big Christmas Eve event. It's a huge party with all our friends and neighbors. It's my favorite thing and I look forward to it all year."

"I know," I said, nodding.

"You know?"

"Yeah," I replied, still nodding. Thinking about the Treloff family holiday celebration always pinched me in a strange way. "You told Shay and Emme, and the rest of the early elementary people, all about it last year. It's the only time you eat ham and only because it's doused in your grandmother's special pineapple sauce."

Her lips quirked up as her brows fell. "How do you know that?"

"How do I know that," I muttered, glancing to the ceiling. I couldn't do this anymore. Whatever I was doing with this woman, it was over. I couldn't hate her, not really and not for pretend either. I wasn't strong enough, not when I knew the feel of her body and the way her skin tasted and all the glorious ways she loved to be snuggled. "How do I know you eat ham on Christmas Eve and have nine pairs of shoes straight from a crayon box and dump fucking cinnamon on your coffee and listen to the *Artemis Fowl* books in audio all the goddamn time? How do I know you're the oldest of three and your next sibling is eight years younger than you, and you were the full-time babysitter in your house by the time you were ten and you've basically been a kindergarten teacher your entire life because of it? Or how do I know that you curse all the time but think no one notices because you do it quietly? How do I know any of this, Tara? *How do I know?* How do I know you like pineapple sauce and why the hell would I devote hours to searching for a recipe even though the only thing I know how to make is reservations? Why would I schedule the parent conferences for your grade levels or try to ban leggings? Why would I wait outside your door with coffee? Why would I die a little when you fell in the snow and then pick you up rather than letting you sort it out on your own?"

She blinked up at me, shook her head. "I—I don't know."

"Because I've been in love with you since the minute I met you," I said, all the frustration of the past two years seared into my words. Her eyes widened, her lips parted. It was a fine reminder I'd done everything in my power to run far and fast from my feelings for her, to be as repellant as possible, to make her hate me so much she didn't notice any of the ways I fawned over her. "I wasn't especially thrilled about it."

"Why not?" she whispered.

I stared at her kiss-swollen lips. I'd never be able to look at her the same way again. I'd never see those lips without thinking of being here with her.

"I had all these reasons. Explanations. It made sense to me, it really did. But now I can't remember any of it. I just knew I didn't want to feel that way."

"You wanted me gone," she replied, heated. "And this has been fun but I'd be a massive fool to think you don't still want that."

"Yeah, I *did*," I admitted. At one time, showing Tara the door was the best option available to me. I didn't want to want her and I wasn't prepared to make room for her in my life. No more than the room she'd already claimed with her quirky voices and rainbow shoes and all that vanilla. "But not anymore. I swear, that's not my intention. You're right; I don't want to deal with early elementary. I'm sorry about—about everything."

"The King of Dartmouth apologizing? Wow." She bobbed her head, her eyes wide as she considered this. "You know, I've tried to give you the benefit of the doubt."

"Oh, did you?" I replied, immediately suspicious of

this announcement. "Really? When was that? When you were inventing Fun-bruary and incinerating my entire school spirit schedule? Or was it when you developed a new observation and debrief cycle protocol and destroyed my perfectly good system of pluses, minuses, and deltas and replaced it with some fucking *glows and grows?* Or generally making the entire staff fall in love with you—myself included—because you're so warm and generous and you make everyone feel like a special sunbeam while I'm busy scheduling the delivery of our quarterly inquiry science kits since I don't do songs and skits and Fun-bruary?"

Lifting her chin and giving me the most ruthless little scowl she could manage, she said, "Yesterday. Coffee station. While you were assessing the milk and sugar situation despite your allegiance to Team Black and Bitter."

"What are you talking about?"

"You didn't like the mix and mingle portion of the morning. You were over there, studying up on sweeteners and trying to avoid the world."

How the fuck had she noticed that? "What are you talking about?" I repeated.

"I tried to save you from that situation." She jerked a shoulder up as if it was perfectly ordinary for her to see straight into my weaknesses and soft spots. "Tried to get between you and the awkward introductions, the small talk. That and the gals angling to be the bread in a Drew sandwich."

"The bread in a—*what?* Now you're just inventing stories the way you invented your Dr. Division character who made *my* fourth graders obsessed with math surgery."

"You really must be more careful about those gray trousers, sweetie. Yesterday was not the first time you had eyes all over your ass. And it wasn't the first time you slaughtered my willingness to give you a chance."

"I don't understand anything you just said," I started, "but I am sorry about how I responded yesterday. At the coffee station. I was a dick and you didn't deserve that."

There. That wasn't so difficult. Truthfully, everything was easier when cozied up in bed with Tara. If needed, I could confess all of my mistakes and errors so long as I could keep both hands on her naked body.

She brought her hand to her chest, which gave me a grand opportunity to study her outrageously perfect curves. "I don't know how to handle all these apologies. I'd like to believe them but—"

"Tell me more about Christmas Eve," I said, resting my head between her breasts because everything was better there. "Tell me about pineapple sauce."

"Why?" she asked, sliding her fingers through my hair. "Why do you want that?"

"Because I don't want to think about the terrible things I've said to you and the inexcusable way I've behaved. I know what I've done. I want to pretend I'm allowed to love you and maybe, in some wild version of my life, you love me too."

"Why aren't you allowed to love me, Drew?"

"Please reference the previously mentioned terrible things and inexcusable behavior. The rules of thought don't allow for those types of incompatible events, not unless you're a true nihilist. Even then, a true nihilist never would've fallen down this rabbit hole. Nah, a nihilist would've walked away a year ago. More. A nihilist would've bailed out after a week of watching you play with your hair every afternoon. Would've known better."

She was silent for a moment, her nails lightly scraping my neck and scalp. Then, "We don't actually do anything on Christmas. That might be weird but I've never thought of it that way. Just a big feast on Christmas Eve and a drunken stumble down the block for midnight mass. That's the part that matters to my mother. She's a purist when it comes to Christmas Eve mass. The rest is flexible." She laughed, twisting my hair around her fingers and tugging just a bit. "You're going to have to be on your best behavior since I've spent two years telling my parents you're a nightmare to work with."

"I can do that," I said because why not keep this imaginary love story going a little longer? I pressed a kiss to the underside of her breast. Fuck, I wanted to live right here. All day, every day, under the sweetest set of tits I'd ever tasted. "You're gonna need to do the same when we fly to Pennsylvania on Christmas morning. I didn't use the word 'nightmare' but I've implied you're a handful." I gave her ass a squeeze for emphasis. "Which is the damn truth."

"You think I'm joking," she said.

"Of course you are," I replied. "We're going to have to leave this cabin or cottage or whatever the fuck it is soon and make our way back to civilization. I know better than to expect this means anything."

She tipped her head back, scowled. "This didn't mean anything to you?"

This was what drowning felt like, right? There was no other explanation I could gather for this overwhelming sense that I could kick and fight but I'd never reach the surface, never properly breathe again. Because there was no way out here. I was the villain in her story.

Even if she'd enjoyed my dick several times last night and this morning, she didn't enjoy *me*.

And I'd fucked up everything with her. If I took a

minute to step back and survey the damage I'd done by being—unfortunately—a full-blast version of myself, it became obvious I couldn't fix any of it. Sharing a bed for one night wasn't going to make up for all the times I'd made her feel small and incompetent—and it shouldn't.

Some good sex didn't heal those wounds.

Because there was no reason to hide anything anymore, I answered, "Tara, sweetheart, I've sliced myself open and bled myself dry in the past eighteen hours. You know exactly what this has meant to me. What I'm saying is I know it doesn't change anything for us because we can't—we don't—"

"I'm taking you home, Drew Larsen. I'm dressing you in an ugly sweater and feeding you ham and introducing you to my parents."

I shifted to face her. "What? How is that going to—I mean—what?"

"What if I just…let you love me? Would that be so bad?"

"It wouldn't be bad at all," I sputtered. "But I don't know if I deserve it."

She shrugged. "You'll earn it."

"Ah. I see. I'll spend the next seven hundred years in your debt. Sounds grand," I murmured.

"That's not what I mean at all," she snapped. "Let's just…start over. From last night. We're both going to do better and be better than we were before this blizzard. We'll earn it, okay?" Before I could offer my resounding agreement or, I didn't know, propose marriage, she continued. "It's not like we'll ever stop fighting, so let's take that off the table right now. And it's not like we're going to agree on every pedagogical issue we encounter. We'll drop that too. But maybe we could channel all the energy we'd devoted to hating each other into something a little"—she wiggled beneath me and my cock perked up with a hearty *Yes, please* —"better?"

"My parents are going to adore you," I said. "They'll have no use for me."

"That's understandable." She pursed her lips, nodding. "You are insufferable."

"I'm going to need you to wear proper winter boots if we're stumbling to church at midnight, Tara," I continued. "My heart cannot take a repeat of last night and I don't know how your family will react to me carrying you to midnight mass."

"I'll agree to boots if you agree to those gray trousers," she said. "We'll need to find a dry cleaner."

"You want to check out my ass that bad?"

"Honey, if you think I haven't been checking out your ass all this time, you haven't been paying attention."

CHAPTER TEN

TARA

IT WAS afternoon by the time we gathered ourselves together and exited the cottage, plus another half hour of assuring the innkeeper we'd managed the night without incident.

I couldn't believe Drew maintained a straight face through that conversation when I had to bite my lip to keep from giggling.

Now we were headed back to Boston, my hands curled around a hot cup of coffee as I settled into the passenger seat beside Drew. The same Drew who kept glancing at me as if he expected me to snap out of it and realize I'd mistakenly given him the green light to be my guy.

Maybe it was a mistake. Maybe I'd have a different mindset on the matter in a few weeks, a few months.

Maybe I was offering him far more than he deserved and it would come back to bite me in the ass and put me out of a job.

And maybe none of that was true.

The absolute facts were limited but I was certain Drew wasn't faking any of this and neither was I. Either we'd learn to work together or we wouldn't.

Because there was no time like the present, I said, "Let's go over the game plan."

"You know the game plan. We're stopping at your apartment first and then—actually, can you settle something for me? Do you have dried macaroni in a jar somewhere? Like, in your living room? For craft projects and shit?"

"I'm not answering that." I waved that question off. "I wasn't referring to our game plan for today. I meant our plan for returning to work in two weeks and being around our friends and colleagues. What's our plan for that?"

I watched as he scanned the highway ahead, only the firm set of his jaw giving away his reaction.

When he didn't respond, I continued, "We need some ground rules."

"Operating procedures."

"Basically, yes. Most of all, we need to be professional."

Drew snorted out a laugh. "Because we've done such an exceptional job at that so far."

He was right on that count, however—"We can't have sex in our office. Or anything in the periphery of sex."

"Oh." That was his only reaction. Then, "Oh. Right. That's what we're talking about."

I peered at him. "What did you think I was referring to?"

He shook his head in the rushed, impatient way he did when he wanted to sweep my comment to the side. "I don't know. Let's just say I don't know what to think about any of this. I'm just happy we moved the holiday party from this weekend to New Year's Day and we don't have to see anyone from school for two weeks because I want you all to myself for once."

My resentment and loathing of Drew Larsen were like a clear sliding glass door and I'd walked into it too many times to count, always staggering away with an egg on my forehead and some wounded pride.

Until he'd kissed me and cracked it right down the middle. After everything we'd shared and experienced together, it was a cobweb of fractures.

And now, with his words simmering between us, that door needed little more than a flick of my fingers to shatter all the way.

"I'm not ready to tell everyone," I started, "but we should tell Lauren. It's the responsible thing to do."

"You're not ready because you're preparing yourself for me to be an ass to you all over again and fuck everything up," he said under his breath.

"I'm not ready because I want us to figure this out without a captive audience," I replied.

"And you're expecting me to be an ass to you," he added.

"Will you?"

Rubbing the back of his neck, he said, "I'm going to try like hell not to."

"All right then." I sipped my coffee, silent as I studied signs along the highway and shoulder-height snow drifts. "Since I know how you feel about benchmarks and metrics and such things, let's establish a target. A goal, if you will."

Drew shot me a sidelong glance before saying, "Go on."

"We'll give this a shot," I said, gesturing between us. "We'll date. We'll meet each other's families and spend time together. We'll be a couple—quietly. I'm not suggesting we sneak around but I don't want the eyeballs of the entire teaching staff on us while we figure this out. And if we like where it's going, we'll make a big announcement at the end-of-year staff party."

"You're giving me almost seven months? That seems generous," he quipped.

"Do you want it or not?" I snapped, a laugh ringing in my words.

He reached over and laced my fingers in his. "I want it."

CHAPTER ELEVEN

TARA

"RAMEN BOWLS?" Drew asked from his end of the sofa as he ran his hands over my ankles and up my legs.

"We had ramen bowls two nights ago," I replied, snuggling deeper into his cozy blanket.

Rather surprisingly, I liked Drew's apartment a lot. It wasn't nearly as cold or impersonal as I'd imagined —although I had imagined him sleeping in a hollowed-out torpedo so anything was an improvement on that.

Much like the blanket he'd kept artfully draped over the back of the sofa, his place was cozy. There were books everywhere, he had a habit of abandoning his ties all over the place, he kept nothing in the refrig-erator—and we'd been holed up here since returning from his hometown several days ago.

We'd even agreed to skip the school's annual holiday party today because we didn't want to forfeit these final hours of couple time before we had to get back to business on Monday.

And we didn't want to put on real clothes.

He regarded me with a slight smile. "Pizza?"

I shook my head with an exaggerated groan. "It's New Year's Day. We're supposed to be eating egg whites and asparagus or…something dreadful like that."

"As you said, sweetheart, dreadful," he replied. "How do you feel about tempura? There's a place Clark turned me onto last year with the best vegetable tempura I've ever had." When his phone buzzed, he reached for it on the coffee table and chuckled. "Speak of the freakin' devil."

"What is it?"

He handed me his phone. "See for yourself."

Clark: Where are you, man? It's the school holiday party. Attendance is basically mandatory and I require a shoulder to commiserate on.

Clark: FFS, I'm here and we all know I'd rather be anywhere but.

Clark: The elementary team is hypothesizing whether you and Treloff finally killed each other. It would be amusing to watch if I wasn't trying to get the hell out of here but that's not happening.

Clark: The problem being, the human shield I brought with me today is now besties with the boss and she's hooking us up with a new science teacher so I'll probably die here.

I shot Drew a confused smile. "What does any of this mean?"

He met me with an equally confused blink. "You don't know?"

Slowly shaking my head, I said, "I understand that both of us skipping that party might raise some eyebrows and start up the rumor mill but what's this about commiserating and human shields?"

He tapped out a quick response and dropped his phone back on the table. "Clark has a thing for Noa. A *significant* thing."

"Does she know that?" I asked, thinking about the middle grade language arts teacher Noa Elbaz.

"Oh, hell no," he replied with a laugh. "No, no, no. She's made it perfectly clear that's a nonstarter and he…well, he's still getting over that rejection. He does a fantastic job of making her believe he's busy being Tinder's top user."

"But—but—they lesson plan together every weekend." I couldn't wrap my mind around this.

"They collaborate on everything. Their pacing is lockstep. They debrief every single class during passing periods. How do they—how does he survive that?"

"It's a cocktail of bitterness and resentment with a chaser of self-flagellation," he replied.

"*Ohhhhh.*" Now I understood. I never would've guessed these men were tender-hearted buddies. "You and Clark both—that's why he needed a shoulder for commiseration."

"Yes." He squeezed my calf. "Clark will make it through without me. There are plenty of people at this event to distract him."

Before I could ask anything else, my phone buzzed—and didn't stop. "Wow," I breathed, reading through messages from Emme Ahlborg, the sorceress of second grade, Audrey Saunders, the fabulous ruler of the fifth graders, and Shay Zucconi, the queen of kindergarten. "The elementary team really does think we killed each other."

Emme: Hey, doll. So, some of our dear friends are worried you've died. Please confirm otherwise.
Audrey: Hi there. We're all here at the holiday party and wondering if you're okay.
Shay: Tara! I thought I was going to see you today at Lauren's! What's up, girlfriend?

Audrey: I'm sure you're all right and everything is fine but you know how I worry.

Shay: Tell the truth—did you and Larsen fight it out cage-match style? And can I hear the gory details?

Emme: If you're busy living your life, please continue doing that. Explanations are unnecessary. Everyone will just have to simmer down.

Audrey: You know I worry a lot. I'm sorry. It's just so unlike you to miss an event and I haven't seen you since before the winter break started.

Emme: Ignore Audrey. I'll deal with her.

When I handed him the device, he scrolled through the messages with a low whistle. "Your team adores you. You've even snatched Audrey out from underneath me."

"You say that like it's a competition. Like it's a knock against you because my team is demonstrably affectionate." I wagged a finger at him. "Everyone adores you. It might not be the same love and sunshine I get but that's because it's what I give them. They adore you in reliable, loyal, tireless ways because that's what you give them."

"Do you?" he asked. "Adore me?"

I pressed my toes against his inner thigh. "I think I might."

CHAPTER TWELVE

TARA

"HAPPY NEW YEAR," Lauren sang as we settled around her conference table on the first day back from winter break. "Even though it's only been two weeks, I feel like I haven't seen you guys in months."

"Again, I'm sorry I couldn't make it to your New Year's Day cookie-and-wine swap party," I said, sneaking a quick glance across the table at Drew. He was frowning at his laptop, completely indifferent to my presence. It was kind of amazing how quickly he slipped back into that mode. "It was such a blast last year. I loved those shortbread cookies you made. I hate that I missed it."

It didn't seem necessary to explain why I'd missed her party and she wasn't pressed for details. Since Drew and I weren't prepared to make this thing we had going public—the new thing, not the old thing where we fantasized about killing each other—and most of our friends were teachers at the school, we'd gorged on (and argued about) takeout, watched (and argued about) movies, drank (and argued about) cheap champagne.

"Well, there's approximately nine million cookies in the workroom if you want to grab some now," she replied. "No wine. That will have to wait until after hours, you know, on account of all the children in the building and the fact it's nine in the morning."

Drew ignored both of us in his pursuit of constant frowning.

"While that is tempting, I had more than enough sugar for breakfast," I replied.

And there it was—the tiniest of smirks from my arch enemy. My nemesis. The man who drove me absolutely fucking crazy and nearly forced me out of this school and my job in the process. The one who smothered me in so much affection, I only stopped smiling to argue with him.

Yeah, we still fought like cats and dogs. That wasn't about to change and I didn't think I'd want that. The basis of our relationship was big, bold disagreement but we didn't hate each other nearly as much as we'd thought.

No, it required trust and openness to really argue with someone. To make strong statements and stand behind them even when that meant risking everything.

Of course, the insults and name-calling didn't make for the model of effective communication but we'd mostly abandoned that practice.

Mostly.

"Let's dig in," Lauren said, opening her notebook. "I'd love to hear about the session in Albany, even though it was cut short. I still can't believe a blizzard blew through like that. I hope it wasn't too tough getting back here."

Drew groaned, shutting his eyes as he rubbed his temples. "We made it out alive. Let's leave it at that."

When Lauren turned a questioning glance toward me, I said, "It was my fault. I wasn't wearing the right shoes for a blizzard."

"Blizzard, light rainfall, what's the difference?" he muttered.

I gave Lauren a quick shrug. "We made it out alive."

She wagged her pen at me and Drew. "Do I sense a change in the tides?"

I glanced across the table as he closed his laptop. My heart was hammering in my chest and my stomach was churning, and I had to unwrap the scarf from around my neck because I was suddenly burning up.

I didn't know how Lauren was going to react to this news.

"Well, Lauren," he started, meeting my gaze with an arched brow and the barest hint of a smile, "the professional development conference yielded some professional...*developments*. I am profoundly happy to report we've reached an understanding."

She stared at him for a moment before swiveling toward me. "You just lost me a bet with my husband."

"I—what?" I asked.

She waved me off, saying, "It doesn't matter. Keep it professional during school hours and whenever you're in the building. If things don't work out—"

"I took her home to Pennsylvania for Christmas after I spent Christmas Eve with her family," Drew interrupted, again occupied with frowning at his computer. "Not working out isn't among the options."

Now, my heart was hammering for a different reason.

"I want to hear those words from Tara," Lauren said with a sharp chuckle.

Smiling across the table, I said, "I can't believe I'm saying it but Drew's right. On this occasion and relating to this topic, I completely agree with him."

CHAPTER THIRTEEN

DREW

"I CAN'T WEAR it right now," Tara insisted as we walked down Beacon Street together. "Everyone will notice *immediately*."

"Then they notice immediately and it's out in the open," I argued. "Fucking finally."

If there was something more agonizing than spending two full months searching for the perfect engagement ring and then another month planning the perfect proposal, it was a fiancée who said *yes* but required we keep it all a secret from the entire goddamn world for two grueling weeks until we could make a big announcement.

I wanted Tara to have everything she desired and I

didn't care what it was—hell, we were moving in together when her lease ended in August and we'd already decided to get married at that inn out in the Berkshires next summer and I didn't gag when I took a sip of her cinnamon-sprinkled lattes anymore. But I wanted to wrap my arms around her in front of our friends and colleagues and shout "Mine."

"We need to make the announcement, Drew," she said. "If they see a ring, they'll go nuts and it will snowball from there. They'll think it's a prank if I say I'm marrying you."

"Well, that's delightful," I grumbled, holding the door to Hops'N'Scotch open for her. "I suppose we're sticking to the original plan then?"

Before stepping inside, she replied, "Yes. You're doing all the end-of-year recognitions, I'm leading the dramatic reenactment of the best moments of this school year plus my special Bayside rendition of "We're All In This Together" from *High School Musical*, and after Lauren gives her big, sappy speeches for the people who are leaving us, you'll jump in with your usual 'Hey, everyone, I have one more thing for the group.' Then I'll put on the ring."

"What do you mean, *my usual*?"

Before she could respond, Max Murphy, the school's gym teacher, stepped through the doorway, saying, "Come on, now, kids. No fighting today. Not unless you want me to organize a dodgeball game to the death. Then again, some carnage might brighten my spirits."

The poor guy was still bruised from a nasty break-up with his cheating boyfriend over the winter. He was unflappable with the kids but there was no mistaking the rain cloud hanging heavy over him these past few months.

As he disappeared into the tavern, she gestured after him. "See? They'd think it's a prank. They still think we can't stand each other and that will make your usual one-more-thing even better."

In truth, we didn't have to work that hard at keeping up our ongoing disagreements. We still had different viewpoints and priorities and methods, and tearing each other's clothes off the minute we got home from work didn't change that. If anything, it made it all the more enjoyable.

"Fine," I muttered. "Let's get this over with."

I followed Tara inside but we promptly split up as we always did, her swallowed up by the elementary teachers and me busying myself with the projector and slide deck to accompany the award portion of these events. Staying busy was the only way to keep this charade going.

If I had time on my hands, I'd spend it gazing at my fiancée and thinking about all the ways she drove me crazy. I'd been caught doing that a time or two and everyone seemed to think I was sick.

If only they knew how wrong they were.

After Tara's extremely goofy but highly adorable performance and Lauren's farewells, I stood, saying, "Could I have one minute? Just one last thing?"

"The next round is on you, Larsen," Max shouted.

I nodded, saying, "I'm on board with that. I think we'll all want to raise a glass after you hear what I have to say." Tara buried her face in her hands, her shoulders shaking with laughter. When she peeked at me through her fingers, I beckoned for her to join me. "Get up here, Treloff."

"Oh my god, what's happening?" Audrey asked.

Emme covered Audrey's hand with hers. "Unwedge your panties. Everything will be all right."

Once Tara joined me at the front of the space, she gestured to the group, saying, "Go ahead then. This is your part. On with it."

Suddenly, I was at a loss for words. I'd planned this out but now I couldn't remember what I intended to say. I couldn't reach the carefully crafted beginning or the smooth transitions I'd drafted. I didn't have the anecdotes or light jokes ready. It was gone. And then—

"I think what Drew wants to say is that this has been a really amazing year for us," Tara said. "We've learned and grown so much as your deans and as educators, and we've grown in some personal ways as well."

She glanced at me and we shared a smile. I couldn't do this anymore, I couldn't stand here and be separate from her. I reached out, clasped her hand.

"Why are mommy and daddy looking at each other that way?" Shay asked. "It's weird."

"I think they're going to arm wrestle now," Max added.

Finally finding my words, I said, "I think you all know I love Bayside. This is the best job in the world and you and our students are family to me, and I suppose it makes good sense I'd fall in love at school." I grinned as Tara released my hand to pluck the ring from her pocket. When it was seated in its proper place, I laced her fingers with mine again. "I asked Miss Treloff to marry me and—it shocked me as much as it's shocking you—she said yes."

To say the crowd went wild would be the understatement of the year. They went completely crazy and swarmed us with hugs, handshakes, and more than a few questions about this being an elaborate joke. I didn't mind those questions at all, not when I could answer them with Tara right beside me.

When the group turned their attention to placing that drink order I was paying for, Clark made his way toward us. Tara was busy listening to Lauren's top two hundred wedding planning tips to notice.

"I hate you," he said with a laugh. "Our friendship is over."

I shrugged, saying, "I never thought this would happen and I couldn't have orchestrated it in a thousand years but it did. Maybe it'll happen for you too."

He dipped his hands into his pockets with a sad shake of his head. "Hmm. Probably not but isn't it pretty to think so?"

I paused, glancing across the tavern as I searched for a response that acknowledged Clark's misery but also kicked his ass into high gear because he wasn't going to change a damn thing if he spent all his time picking up women on dating apps and throwing them in Noa's face.

Instead of finding the words, I found Noa leaning against the bar—and watching Clark.

"Don't give up just yet," I said. "You never know when a blizzard will strand you in the Berkshires with just one bed."

"Fuck, I wish," he howled, slapping me on the back before trotting off to drown his sorrows.

"Is he all right?" Tara whispered.

I nodded and kissed her temple. "He will be."

"Are you all right?" she asked.

I folded her into my arms and felt years of tension finally, thoroughly fall away. "I am now."

***

Thank you for reading! I hope you loved Drew and Tara's journey, and the rest of the Bayside family.

Max Murphy is working hard at mending his broken heart. Keep reading for a snippet from Orientation.

If you're ready to go back in time to where it all started, Underneath It All *introduces Matt and Lauren as she worked to open Bayside School. Keep reading for an excerpt!*

Join my newsletter for new release alerts, exclusive extended epilogues and bonus scenes, and more—including future books featuring Bayside School couples (cough cough Clark and Noa)!

Visit my private reader group, Kate Canterbary's Tales, for exclusive giveaways, sneak previews of upcoming releases, and book talk.

The Santillian Triplets

The Magnolia Chronicles — Magnolia

Boss in the Bedsheets — Ash and Zelda

The Belle and the Beard — Linden and Jasper-Anne

Talbott's Cove

Fresh Catch — Owen and Cole

Hard Pressed — Jackson and Annette

Far Cry — Brooke and JJ

Rough Sketch — Gus and Neera

Benchmarks Series

Professional Development — Drew and Tara

Orientation — Jory and Max

Brothers In Arms

Missing In Action — Wes and Tom

Coastal Elite — Jordan and April

Get exclusive sneak previews of upcoming releases through Kate's newsletter and private reader group, The Canterbary Tales, on Facebook.

When Shay Zucconi's step-grandmother died, she left Shay a tulip farm—under two conditions.

First, Shay has to move home to the small town of Friendship, Rhode Island. Second—and most problematic since her fiancé just called off the wedding —Shay must be married within one year.

Marriage is the last thing in the world Shay wants but she'll do anything to save the only real home she's ever known.
Noah Barden loved Shay Zucconi back in high school. Not that he ever told her. He was too shy, too awkward, too painfully uncool to ask out the beautiful, popular girl.

A lifetime later, Noah is a single dad to his niece and has his hands full running the family business. That old crush is the farthest thing from his mind.

Until Shay returns to their hometown and turns his life upside down.

In a Jam — available now!

WILL MAX LOVE AGAIN?
AN EXCERPT FROM ORIENTATION

A KNOCK SOUNDED BEHIND ME, and then, "Is this a bad time?"

Oh my god. I dropped my hands and jerked out of my chair with a force that sent it crashing into a tower of stacked soccer nets. They skittered to the side, knocking over a pillar of orange safety cones and a bag of softballs, sending both straight for Jory's head.

"What is wrong with me?" I panted, diving in front of him to snatch the bag and steady the cones before they flattened him on the floor. I gained control of the equipment before it could do any damage, but I'd also shaved a few years off my life.

"Sorry. Didn't mean to sneak up on you like that." Jory folded his lips together and blinked away from me. "Thanks for intervening, though. You've got some reflexes."

I settled my hands on my waist and blew out a ragged breath. "I didn't hear anything you just said because I'm still reliving the moment when a sack of softballs went flying toward your head."

Orientation is now available!

Max Murphy's no-fail plan for kicking this year's ass and getting his life back on track:

1. Forget about the cheating ex. Forget all about him. No more sad sack moping. None of that downer vibe. None of it.

2. Look for a new place to live in order to move out of my sister's basement. Free digs are great but killing my sex life.

3. Return the intramural softball league to glory and greatness.

4. Fall in fresh, lusty love with Jory Hayzer, the hot new science teacher the minute I see him and his sexy Superman hair.

5. Get the hot science teacher on my trivia team. Couples who play together stay together.

6. Spend an entire school year wooing the very hot but also very skittish science teacher. Fall in hard, crazy love with him in the process.

7. Freak out, screw it all up, and hope to hell there's a way to make it right.

AN EXCERPT FROM UNDERNEATH IT ALL

If you're ready to see where it all started, you'll love Matt and Lauren in *Underneath It All*. **Enjoy this excerpt!**

Fog wafted over Atlantic Avenue as Matthew and I embarked on the short walk to his building. Dipping my toes in the coupled pond—even if it was just for tonight—was wonderfully satisfying. I expected some relief from the constant fix-up attempts, but I never expected to feel so whole, so completely and thoroughly myself standing next to Matthew. But for every ounce of satisfaction, there was an equal amount of hesitation.

"I like your friends." Matthew shrugged, and he couldn't hold back a smug smile.

While most of my friends expressed some appreciation for the beauty that was Matthew Walsh, only Elsie set my teeth on edge. She went in for the hug instead of the handshake, and wrapped her hands around his bicep while she talked about some remodeling she and her husband, Kent, were considering.

I had no business being possessive or territorial or even jealous, but I was. At this moment, Matthew was with me, and she was a little too grabby for my liking.

I rolled my eyes. "My friends liked you, all right. They wanted to drag you out back and take turns on you. Do you always have that effect on married women?"

Matthew stopped in front of the marina outside his building and wrapped his arms around my shoulders, his face taking on a happy, serene quality that seemed unusual for him. "Marry me and find out."

"For the love of tiny purple ponies, Matthew."

I laughed and pushed out of his arms. If I didn't get out of these shoes soon, I was taking them off and walking down the street barefoot. According to the Commodore, that was the best way to pick up gangrene and lose a foot, and a girl needed both feet and all ten toes. He was also fundamentally opposed to my heels (too difficult to flee when the situation demanded it), necklaces (an invitation for strangula-tion), and long hair (something else attackers could grab).

"Is that a yes?"

"You really are a caveman," I said. "I'm tired, I'm cold, my feet hurt, I have to pee, and I want to be out of this dress and eating this cake"—I held up the leftovers from the party—"in the next ten minutes, and we agreed to drinks."

"And my cock in your mouth." He stretched his arm and peered at his watch. He nodded, and said, "By the way: when will that be starting?"

"Sometime after I change and go to the bathroom. And I really do want this cake."

He sighed. "Then we need to talk about citrus fruit."

Grabbing his hand, I towed him inside. "I'm not even going to ask what that means, Matthew."

He leaned against the elevator walls and crossed his arms, his brows pinched in thought. He didn't speak again until we reached his floor. "But I'm a little wounded you turned down my proposal. That shit was heartfelt."

Underneath It All **is available now!**

One hot architect. One naughty schoolteacher. One crazy night that changes everything.

Meet Lauren Halsted.

It's all the little things—the action plans, the long-kept promises—that started falling apart when my life slipped into controlled chaos.

After I fell ass-over-elbow into Matthew Walsh's arms.

Meet Matthew Walsh.

A rebellious streak ran through Lauren Halsted. It was fierce and unrelentingly beautiful, and woven through too many good girl layers to count. She wasn't letting anyone tell her what to do.

Unless, of course, she was naked.

ABOUT KATE

USA Today Bestseller Kate Canterbary writes smart, steamy contemporary romances loaded with heat, heart, and happy ever afters. Kate lives on the New England coast with her husband and daughter.

You can find Kate at www.katecanterbary.com

facebook.com/kcanterbary

instagram.com/katecanterbary

amazon.com/Kate-Canterbary

bookbub.com/authors/kate-canterbary

goodreads.com/Kate_Canterbary

tiktok.com/@katecanterbary

www.ingramcontent.com/pod-product-compliance
Lightning Source LLC
Chambersburg PA
CBHW030816200726
48288CB00004B/1263